The door to her bedroom was ajar. Elizabeth nudged it all the way open.

She blinked. Clothes pulled out of the dresser drawers, pillows tossed about, her desk and closet in total disarray. . . .

Elizabeth clutched the door. Her knees were weak. She tried to call Todd's name, but no sound came out.

"Liz, what's the matter?" Todd asked when he came up and saw her pale face.

"My room has been ransacked. It's just like what happened to the darkroom at school," Elizabeth said with quiet conviction. "They were here, the men from the beach, trying to find the photograph. When they didn't find it in the darkroom, they tracked me home somehow." It was an awful thought. She hadn't found them yet, but they had found her!

Bantam Books in the Sweet Valley High series
Ask your bookseller for the books you have missed

SWEET VALLEY HIGH

REGINA'S LEGACY

Written by
Kate William

Created by
FRANCINE PASCAL

BANTAM BOOKS
NEW YORK · TORONTO · LONDON · SYDNEY · AUCKLAND

RL 6, IL age 12 and up

REGINA'S LEGACY
A Bantam Book / March 1991

Sweet Valley High is a registered trademark of Francine Pascal

Conceived by Francine Pascal

Produced by Daniel Weiss Associates, Inc.
33 West 17th Street
New York, NY 10011

Cover art by James Mathewuse

ISBN 0-553-28863-6

Published simultaneously in the United States and Canada

Bantam Books are published by Bantam Books, a division of Bantam Doubleday Dell Publishing Group, Inc. Its trademark, consisting of the words "Bantam Books" and the portrayal of a rooster, is Registered in U.S. Patent and Trademark Office and in other countries. Marca Registrada. Bantam Books, 666 Fifth Avenue, New York, New York 10103.

PRINTED IN THE UNITED STATES OF AMERICA

OPM   0 9 8 7 6 5 4 3 2 1

Dedicated to Yocheved Kurz

One

"I just don't see the attraction of the photography club," Jessica Wakefield confessed to her twin sister, Elizabeth, after school on Wednesday. Jessica was on her way to cheerleading practice while Elizabeth was heading to a meeting of the new Sweet Valley High photography club. "It seems to me that if you were going to take the trouble to join a club, you should have gone for something a little more exciting." Jessica shook a finger at Elizabeth. "I'd better keep my eye on you, Liz. Next thing you know, you'll be trying out for the chess club!"

Elizabeth laughed. Trust Jessica to think of being in the chess club—or having a sister who was—as a fate worse than death. "Don't worry," Elizabeth promised, her eyes sparkling. "I only do one new thing at a time. I'm not joining the chess club until *next* week."

Jessica stopped with Elizabeth at the door to the room where the photography club meetings were held. She peeked inside. "Geek city," she whispered. "No fun hanging around in the darkroom with any of *those* guys!"

"You're terrible," Elizabeth whispered back. "Get out of here!"

"I'm on my way." Jessica waltzed off down the corridor toward the gym. "Wouldn't want to linger too long in the vicinity of such dullness," she remarked over her shoulder. "It might be contagious!"

Elizabeth waved Jessica off. Her sister liked teasing her about being too serious, but Elizabeth knew it was just a question of relativity. Almost everyone seemed too serious compared to Jessica!

On the outside, the sixteen-year-old twins were mirror images of each other, but their personalities were far from identical. They were both blond and slender with blue-green eyes and Southern California suntans. For Jessica, sunbathing was an end in itself; Elizabeth's tan was more incidental, a result of doing her homework by the family swimming pool. Elizabeth believed in a balance of work and play, and she enjoyed her classes as well as being a regular contributor to the Sweet Valley High newspaper, *The Oracle*. Jessica, on the other hand, always put recreation first. When it came to homework or chores, *her* philosophy was not to put off until tomorrow what she could put off until the day after that. Who could study when there were stores to shop in, parties to go to, boys to flirt with, and a telephone to talk on?

Elizabeth didn't think it was such a bad thing to be serious. Keeping a journal and writing her newspaper column, "Eyes and Ears," were important steps toward achieving her goal of becoming a professional writer. And Elizabeth suspected that someday, when her twin discovered what it was *she* wanted more than anything else in the world, Jessica would find out she had a serious side, too.

"Hi, Liz," Olivia Davidson called as Elizabeth entered the room where the photography club was meeting.

"Hi," Elizabeth said as she took the empty chair between Olivia and Patty Gilbert. "Are you two as hooked as I am on this photography stuff?"

"I haven't put my camera down for days," Patty confessed.

"Me, neither," Olivia said. "I'd like to start taking some of my own pictures to go with my articles for *The Oracle*." Olivia was the arts editor of the newspaper.

"Me, too. That's one of the reasons I joined the club." Elizabeth already knew how to develop black-and-white film, but she wanted to learn more advanced techniques. Photography could add a new dimension to her abilities as a journalist.

"Are you trying to put us out of business?" joked Tina Ayala, a staff photographer for *The Oracle*.

"Don't worry. It will take Liz and me years to catch up with you and Allen," Olivia assured Tina.

Elizabeth smiled across the table at Allen Walters. "I'm definitely no threat. I just developed a roll of film, and every single photo is out of focus!"

"You'll get the hang of it," Allen said reassuringly.

The chairs were filling up fast. Current events instructor Mr. Marks, the photography club's faculty adviser, came in followed by Claire Middleton and Andrea Slade. Elizabeth was glad to see Claire and Andrea, both of whom were relatively new members of the Sweet Valley High junior class. Claire had jumped right into the thick of things by being the first girl ever to try out for the football team.

Elizabeth knew that Andrea had tried to keep a low profile, however. She had been wary at first about letting her new friends know that her father was rock star Jamie Peters.

"Is it too late to join?" Claire asked Jim Roberts, the photography buff who had organized the club.

"Nope. This is just our second week."

"I don't know very much about photography," admitted Andrea.

"We've got a lot of beginners," Mr. Marks said. "So our Monday meetings are for instruction. Jim teaches the beginners, and Allen works with people who are ready to move beyond the basics. On Wednesdays, anything goes."

As DeeDee Gordon, Neil Freemount, and Andy Jenkins hurried in and grabbed the last few empty chairs, Elizabeth relaxed. At the last meeting she had overheard John Pfeifer, sports editor for the school paper, telling Allen and Tina that Jeffrey French, another *Oracle* staff photographer, probably wouldn't be able to join the club because of daily soccer team practices. It looked as if John had gotten the story right, and Elizabeth was relieved. She and Jeffrey had been dating when Elizabeth's first love and current boyfriend, Todd Wilkins, moved back to Sweet Valley from Vermont. Breaking up with Jeffrey had been painful, and she was still a little uncomfortable around him.

"Before we head into the darkroom, let's have a look at what everyone's working on," suggested Mr. Marks.

Elizabeth handed her out-of-focus photographs to Patty; in turn, Patty handed her photos to Elizabeth. Patty's pictures were of dancers at the academy where she took ballet and jazz classes. She had had them developed and printed at a lab in town because the school wasn't set up to do color. "These are beautiful," Elizabeth breathed. "They remind me of Degas paintings."

"Do you really think so?" Patty looked pleased. "That was the effect I was aiming for."

DeeDee Gordon, Patty's best friend and an artist, leaned forward to see. "Liz is right. They're wonderful, Pat."

"There are a lot of first-rate photographs here," Mr. Marks observed. "We should really come up with a way to show our stuff to the rest of the school. Maybe the club needs a project, something we can concentrate on and that will get us recognition from the school at the same time."

"We could print some of our pictures in *The Oracle*," Allen suggested. "You know, like 'Guest Photographer of the Week.' "

"That's a good idea," said Jim. "But a group project might be more fun. Something we could work on together."

DeeDee leaned forward, her elbows on the table and her eyes bright with inspiration. "The other day I made a collage out of some of my pictures. What if the club worked on a giant collage? A sort of mural."

"That would be cool!" Andy exclaimed.

"But what would it be about?" asked Neil. "We need some kind of unifying theme."

"It could be about life at Sweet Valley High," Elizabeth suggested. "We could create a photo essay."

Mr. Marks nodded. "I think we're on to something here. A photo essay in the form of a mural would be a great gift to the school right now."

Elizabeth knew what Mr. Marks meant. Not long ago, some racist incidents had disturbed the usually tranquil surface of Sweet Valley High, forcing everyone at the school to confront some very difficult issues. Neil Freemount and Andy Jenkins had been pulled into the center of the turmoil, and their friendship had deteriorated. Elizabeth was glad to see that even though the two boys were no longer as close as they had been, they were still able to participate in the same school activities, such as the new photography club, and to treat each other with respect.

Elizabeth wasn't the only one thinking about those recent problems. "There *has* been some division in the school," said Patty. "The photo essay could be a way of pulling us all back together."

"It would be great for school spirit," Olivia concurred.

"Everyone in the club has different interests, a unique angle on Sweet Valley High," observed Andy.

"Right. And we'd put all those perspectives together. It would be like a tapestry," said DeeDee.

"I think we have a consensus," Mr. Marks declared. "A photo essay it is!"

"Let's keep our project a secret from the rest of the school until it's unveiled," Jim said with a conspiratorial grin.

There was enthusiastic assent. "OK then, it's settled. Let's aim for two weeks from Monday," Mr. Marks decided. "We'll put the collage together over the preceding weekend."

The club members spent the rest of the time discussing various subjects for the mural. Each person had his or her own ideas. Elizabeth could hardly wait to start shooting. It would be fun—and maybe enlightening—to see what kind of Sweet Valley High their cameras discovered!

"I'm never going to be able to memorize all these formulas," Enid Rollins moaned, slamming her textbook shut.

"You always say that when you're studying for a math quiz," Elizabeth pointed out to her best friend, "and you always get A's!"

Enid's green eyes crinkled in a smile. "True. I guess complaining like that is a good luck charm."

"Then maybe I should try it. I have a French quiz tomorrow." In an imitation of Enid, Elizabeth slammed her book shut and declared, "I'll never be able to memorize all these verbs!"

It was Thursday afternoon and the two girls were studying and sunbathing beside the Wakefields' swimming pool. Just as Elizabeth reopened her French book, the phone rang. She hopped up from the chaise longue, dashed through the sliding doors, and hurried into the kitchen to answer the call. "Hello?"

"May I speak to Elizabeth?"

"This is she."

"Elizabeth, it's Skye Morrow."

"Mrs. Morrow! How are you?"

"Quite well, and happy to catch you at

9

home. As I mentioned last week, I have something of Regina's I'd like to give you. I'm sorry I couldn't come by over the weekend as I'd promised. Can I stop by this afternoon?"

"Of course," Elizabeth said. "Whenever you want."

"How about within the next twenty minutes?"

"That would be fine," Elizabeth replied warmly. "I'll see you soon!"

Elizabeth returned to the poolside and told Enid about the phone call. Enid raised her eyebrows. "Mrs. Morrow? Why would she call you?"

"It's kind of mysterious. She's coming over to give me something that belonged to Regina, but I don't know what it is."

"I wonder what it could be?"

Elizabeth wondered, too, as she pulled her T-shirt on over her bathing suit and stepped into her shorts. Skye Morrow was the mother of Elizabeth's friend Nicholas, a recent Sweet Valley High graduate who was dating Andrea Slade. Elizabeth told Enid about having run into Mrs. Morrow in downtown Sweet Valley the previous week. "It had been ages since I'd seen her," Elizabeth mused. "In fact, I think the last time was . . ." Her voice trailed off, and a pained expression clouded her face.

"Regina's funeral?" Enid said quietly.

Elizabeth nodded sadly.

It was a very sad time for Elizabeth. Nicholas Morrow's younger sister Regina had been a junior at Sweet Valley High and a good friend. Upset because her boyfriend had left her for another girl, Regina impetuously took up with a bad crowd. At a party she was pressured into trying cocaine, and she died from a rare reaction to the drug.

The Wakefields' golden Labrador retriever, Prince Albert, had been snoozing in the sun. Now he pricked up his ears and barked as he heard a car in the driveway. "That must be Mrs. Morrow now."

"I'll stay out here," Enid offered.

Elizabeth reached the front door just as Mrs. Morrow rang the bell. She greeted her friend's mother with a warm smile. "Come on in!"

Mrs. Morrow stepped into the hall, and Elizabeth noticed she was carrying a small box. "Why don't we sit in the living room?" she suggested. "Can I get you anything first? A glass of iced tea?"

"No, thank you," Mrs. Morrow said. "I can only stay a minute."

As she sat down on the couch and faced Mrs. Morrow, Elizabeth couldn't help but picture Regina. Skye Morrow had been a model once,

11

and she was still very beautiful. Regina had had her mother's long, wavy black hair and her dark, dramatic eyes. Elizabeth felt a lump form in her throat, but she willed herself to smile brightly. She didn't want Mrs. Morrow to know she was thinking melancholy thoughts about Regina.

Elizabeth couldn't fool the older woman. Mrs. Morrow put her hand on Elizabeth's. "I know you miss Regina," she said softly. "We do, too. The months since her death . . . In all my life, time has never seemed to pass so slowly."

Now it was Elizabeth's turn to squeeze Mrs. Morrow's hand. "I'm sure it's been difficult."

Mrs. Morrow sighed. "At first, I wanted to leave Regina's room just as it was, but now I'm trying to be practical. Mr. Morrow and I are going to donate Regina's clothes and books to charities, but as I was going through her belongings I came across something I thought you'd like to have—and something I know Regina would have liked you to have."

Mrs. Morrow handed the box to Elizabeth.

A photograph was taped to the lid of the box. As Elizabeth gazed at it, the lump returned to her throat. The picture was of Regina and her. "I remember this day. It was Regina's sixteenth birthday party."

Mrs. Morrow nodded. "Her father and I had given her a new camera."

"Mr. Morrow used it to take the picture," Elizabeth recalled.

"That's right." Mrs. Morrow smiled. "Go ahead. Open the box."

Elizabeth had a hunch she knew what was inside. She was right: it was the camera. "Oh, Mrs. Morrow, it's beautiful. This is so generous of you! I don't know what to say."

"Andrea was over with Nicholas yesterday, and she told me about the new photography club at school. She mentioned that you had joined," Mrs. Morrow explained. "I knew then that I had been right in wanting to give the camera to you. Regina was getting so interested in photography. Her father had built a dark-room in the basement for her, and she was just learning to develop her own pictures when she died." Mrs. Morrow's dark eyes grew misty.

"It's a lovely gift," Elizabeth whispered. She knew it must be hard for Mrs. Morrow to part with a possession that had been so precious to her daughter. At the same time, Elizabeth saw that by giving away Regina's things, Mrs. Morrow was slowly coming to terms with her grief. "Thank you, Mrs. Morrow."

"It will mean a lot to me to know that you're enjoying the camera."

"I'll take good care of it," Elizabeth promised her.

Elizabeth stood at the door and waved as Mrs. Morrow drove off. Then she went back to the living room and took the camera from its black leather case. For a long moment, she just held it and thought about Regina. Then she went back to the pool to rejoin Enid and show her the camera.

Two

"Mind if we join you?" Elizabeth asked Shelley Novak and Jim Roberts in the cafeteria on Monday.

Shelley welcomed Elizabeth and Todd with a broad smile. "Of course not!" She shot a playful look at Jim. "I *had* thought maybe we'd have a quiet lunch, just the two of us, but I should have known. There's always a third party. His camera!"

Jim patted the camera, which was sitting on the table next to his lunch tray. "Sorry, Shell. I've had this camera a lot longer than I've had you."

"What if I carried my basketball with me everywhere I went?" Shelley asked. "Wouldn't that drive you crazy?"

"Maybe you don't carry it with you all the time, but you're as wacky about basketball as I am about photography," Jim countered. "Tell me I'm right, Liz. Aren't basketball nuts the worst?"

Elizabeth looked at her boyfriend. Tall, handsome Todd Wilkins was the star forward for the boys' basketball team. "Definitely the worst," Elizabeth joked.

"These two have no compassion for the life of an athlete," Todd told Shelley. "And I know what you mean about all this picture taking. I used to worry about Liz *writing* things about me. She has a notebook and pencil with her all the time. Now I've got to watch out for her camera, too. Just when I think I can relax and be myself, she's pointing it at me again."

"Oh, please," Elizabeth laughed. "You love it. Don't deny it. You're always posing!"

Todd grinned. "I just figure if you're going to take pictures of me, they might as well be good ones."

"I wouldn't mind if Jim only took pictures of me," said Shelley, twisting the stem off her apple. "Although I used to hate it."

Elizabeth knew Shelley had once been very self-conscious, particularly about her height, even though she was very pretty. She'd been known to yell at the photographers, including

Jim, who took pictures of her when she was on the court with the girls' basketball team. Since she had started dating Jim, however, Shelley seemed to have grown more comfortable with herself.

"But it's *not* just me he takes pictures of," Shelley continued. "Lately he's been taking pictures of every other person who crosses his path. Look! There he goes again!"

Jim had been gazing around the crowded cafeteria with a speculative eye. Suddenly he had grabbed his camera, twisted in his chair, focused the zoom lens, and snapped a picture.

Shelley shook her head. "All I see is Winston Egbert trying to balance his lunch tray on his head. Why would you bother taking a picture of something as silly as that?"

Jim smiled mysteriously and caught Elizabeth's eye. She took a bite of her sandwich to keep from giggling.

Todd observed this exchange. "What goes on in this photography club, anyway?"

"We take pictures," Jim replied neutrally.

"And develop and print them," Elizabeth added innocently.

"I should have warned you," Shelley said to Todd. "The first time Liz picked up a camera, she was doomed. It does something to the brain."

"Don't worry about us," Elizabeth assured

Todd and Shelley. "We're not as cracked as we seem!" She took another bite of her sandwich and enjoyed Todd's quizzical look. Jim's idea to make the photo essay a secret had certainly made the project more fun. Now, if they could only *keep* it a secret!

Jim, Elizabeth, and a few other members of the photography club stayed late in the darkroom Monday afternoon. The darkroom was Jim's favorite spot at Sweet Valley High. He loved everything about it: the enlargers and basins for processing prints, the new print dryer, even the way the orange safelight cast a warm glow on the photographers' faces.

"How many pictures did you take this past weekend?" Jim asked as Elizabeth clipped up another long strip of negatives to dry.

"Three rolls of thirty-six," Elizabeth confessed. "I don't know what came over me! I got in my car on Saturday morning and spent the whole day driving around Sweet Valley. Everywhere I looked, I saw a picture waiting to be taken. I couldn't stop myself."

"I recognize this phenomenon." Jim grinned. "It's called photo-obsession."

"And you should know!"

"It's true," Jim conceded. "Ever since I got

18

my first camera when I was a kid, it's been like a part of my body. Shelley's right—I take it with me everywhere."

"So you formed the club as an outlet for your artistic energy," DeeDee surmised.

"I guess. Except if anything, it's increased my obsession. This photo essay's really gotten me in gear. Although I'm still looking for a special angle."

"The only thing I'm sure of is that I'm going to stick to black-and-white for this project," Elizabeth said. "I'm still not completely confident working with color, and I don't want to goof up."

"I'm just worried my pictures won't be good enough for the mural." Andrea looked over at Jim. "Is this what I do next?"

"You've got it," Jim confirmed. "Just slide the print into the developer and agitate it. Then after two minutes, put it in the stop bath for thirty seconds." He went on to explain the timing for the fixer and the wash.

Andrea did as Jim instructed. A minute later, she gave an excited squeal. "Look at my picture!"

Jim smiled. It was the first photo Andrea had printed on her own. He knew how excited she felt.

Elizabeth peered at the photograph floating

19

in the developer and burst out laughing. "What a riot!"

Andrea had taken a picture of her rock-star father doing a cannonball off the diving board of their swimming pool. "In private, my dad's kind of a goof," Andrea confided.

"By the way, Liz," said Jim. "Is that a new camera you have?"

"Yes. It's inspired me. That's one of the reasons I've been taking more pictures than ever. Here, check it out."

Elizabeth took the camera from its case and handed it to Jim. He examined it with an expert's eye and whistled in admiration. "This is the best camera Nikon makes. If it was a gift, somebody must really like you."

"Actually, it was." Elizabeth told the others about her visit from Regina Morrow's mother.

"Mrs. Morrow was glad she had something to give you to remember Regina by," Andrea affirmed.

Elizabeth tipped her head thoughtfully. "It's funny, but when I use the camera, I feel close to Regina. It's almost as if she's with me, as if when I look through the lens I'm seeing the world with Regina's eyes as well as my own. Does that sound weird?"

Claire looked up from placing a piece of printing paper on the easel of an enlarger. "No, it doesn't," she said softly. "After Ted died . . ." Claire paused. She seemed far away at that moment, obviously thinking about her older brother who had died of cancer shortly before the Middletons moved to Sweet Valley. "He still seemed alive in my memory," Claire continued. "I felt his presence when I tried out for the football team. Whenever I threw a pass it was like my arms got strength from him."

"The photography club must seem kind of tame after football," Jim remarked.

Claire smiled. "Working on the photo essay is exciting in a different way."

"Just watch out for nosy people," Elizabeth warned. "Jim and I are already having a tough time keeping this a secret."

"Speaking of nosy people, I have to meet Shelley," Jim announced with a laugh. "I'm out of here."

"I'm done, too," said Elizabeth. "I'll walk out with you."

"Stick around as long as you want," Jim told the others. "Just make sure the last person out locks the darkroom door. And hide any photo-essay evidence!"

Shelley stood in front of the locker room mirror and towel-dried her hair. Then she combed

21

it out with her fingers, leaving it attractively tousled.

"Ready to head out, Shell?" her best friend Cathy Ulrich asked.

"Um-hmm. I just need to grab my book bag from my locker."

"It was a pretty good practice," Cathy commented as they left the locker room.

"Yeah," Shelley agreed. "After that killer season with the team, intramurals are a lot of fun."

"You can't fool me," Cathy teased her. "You still play to win."

Shelley grinned. "I never said I didn't!"

"Where are you off to? I have my mom's car today, so I could drop you off somewhere."

"Thanks, but I'm meeting up with Jim. Guess where *he* is?"

Cathy pretended to ponder the question and Shelley laughed. "I'll just take a wild guess. The darkroom?"

"Bingo!"

The two girls said goodbye, and Shelley hurried in the direction of the darkroom. It was silly. She had seen Jim only a few hours ago, but she missed him as much as if they'd been separated for a week. Shelley had always thought the feeling she got playing basketball was the best feeling in the world. But that was before she fell in love with Jim.

She entered the photography-club room just as Jim emerged from the darkroom with Elizabeth. They were deep in conversation.

"Well, hello you two," Shelley remarked dryly. "It's a good thing I'm not the jealous type, Jim, or I'd wonder about you spending afternoons in a darkroom with beautiful blondes."

"You don't have to worry." Jim reassured her as he slipped his arm around her waist.

"With Jim and me, it's just a meeting of minds," Elizabeth explained.

"You mean a meeting of lenses!" Shelley kidded.

Elizabeth stopped off at the *Oracle* office. Jim and Shelley strolled toward the lobby, their arms around each other's waists. "So, how's Sweet Valley High's latest extracurricular craze?" Shelley asked.

"People are lining up in droves to join," Jim joked. "Seriously, though, we've got a lot more members than I expected. I think the club's going to be a big success."

"Of course it is." Shelley hugged her boyfriend a little bit closer. "With you in charge, it has to be."

"Flattery will get you everywhere!"

"So, let's see today's batch of pictures." Shelley could barely contain her curiosity.

"Pictures?"

"Yeah, pictures." Shelley tickled his waist. "You know, those things you take with your camera. That *is* what the photography club's for, isn't it, taking pictures?"

"I don't have any with me," said Jim with a shrug.

Shelley tapped her finger on the manila folder he was carrying. "Then what's in here?"

Jim quickly stuck the folder inside one of his books. "Sorry, that's classified information."

"Come on," she pressed. "I just want to see what you're working on these days. What's wrong with that?"

"Nothing, but—"

"So, hand it over!" She was beginning to get annoyed.

With one arm, Jim held his books away from her, and with the other he pulled her to him for a kiss. "You'll just have to take my word for it, Shell. You don't want to see these pictures."

"OK, but I don't know why *these* particular pictures should be such a big deal."

"You'll understand one of these days," Jim assured her.

Jim's car was one of the last left in the student parking lot. Shelley climbed into the passenger seat, only half listening to Jim as he talked about the movie they were planning to see at the Valley Cinema that night. Her mind was still on the manila folder and its mysterious contents.

What was Jim hiding, and why?

Three

"No way, Liz. You're not taking the car again!" Jessica protested the next afternoon as Elizabeth entered the kitchen, her camera bag over one shoulder and the keys to the Fiat in her hand. "I'm going shopping today."

"You're just going to the mall with Lila, aren't you? She can drive," Elizabeth pointed out reasonably.

Jessica stepped in between Elizabeth and the door, blocking her twin's escape route. "Lila said it was my turn to drive, and she's right. When Mom and Dad gave us the car, we were supposed to share it, remember? And you've been monopolizing it for your boring photography project."

"Maybe I have, but who's the one who *usually*

26

hogs it to go to the mall all the time?" Elizabeth countered.

Jessica put her hands on her hips. "I do not go to the mall all the time!"

"I'll tell you what. I'll drop you off at the mall on my way to the beach to take pictures, and then I'll pick you up on my way back."

"Thanks anyway," Jessica said with a sniff, "but I'll get a ride with Lila. As usual." She narrowed her eyes. "All I can say is this photography club is really getting out of hand. At first I thought it was just you. You have to admit, it's not normal to take a picture of Ms. Dalton in the middle of French class!"

Elizabeth had decided on her special angle for the mural just that morning: she would photograph Sweet Valley High teachers doing what they did best. Ms. Dalton had been her first subject. Elizabeth smiled. "I asked her before class if it was OK. But who else is acting weird?"

"That nerd Allen Walters," continued Jessica. "He snuck into cheerleading practice today and was zooming in at us from all over the place! I thought he was only interested in math and chemistry. You photography-club types are just a bunch of Peeping Toms. It gives me the creeps!"

"One of these days it won't seem so creepy,"

Elizabeth promised her sister. "Happy shopping!"

"Happy snooping," Jessica retorted as Elizabeth headed outside.

Elizabeth supposed she couldn't blame her twin for being a little annoyed about her taking the car. She was guilty as charged. Lately, she had been spending all her free time taking pictures with Regina's camera both during and after school.

"And today we're going to the beach," Elizabeth said to Prince Albert, who had followed her out of the house. Prince Albert barked happily when he realized Elizabeth was going to take him along in the car. He jumped right into the small back area, not even waiting for Elizabeth to open the door to the convertible.

Elizabeth drove at a leisurely pace, humming to the songs on the radio. It was another perfect Southern California day. The sky was clear and blue, and palm trees waved in the gentle breeze. As Elizabeth crested a hill, she caught a glimpse of the Pacific. A short time later, she was parking the Fiat in the lot next to one of the public beaches. She had deliberately chosen a different beach than the one where the Sweet Valley students hung out. Instead, she chose a deserted beach, one where there was no swimming.

Camera in hand, Elizabeth walked barefoot onto the sand. She loved the beach. It was so much a part of life in Sweet Valley. She couldn't have counted the number of times she had come there for a quiet time with just one friend or for a volleyball game or a cookout with a whole crowd. Now Elizabeth recalled a few parties in particular, given back when Regina was still alive. She had always brightened the scene with her beautiful smile.

I was lucky to have a friend like Regina, she thought. Elizabeth lifted the camera to her eye and focused on a big piece of polished and fancifully twisted driftwood. She also snapped a few pictures of Prince Albert chasing seagulls. Then Elizabeth sat down by the driftwood. She knew she was partially hidden and hoped to catch a few beachcombers unaware.

She smiled as she waited for her first victim. Maybe Jessica was right. Maybe she *was* turning into a Peeping Tom!

After several minutes, Elizabeth stood up and stretched. She walked along the beach, snapping pictures every few minutes. She photographed a funny old man in a straw hat, searching for treasure in the sand with a metal detector; a long-haired surfer waiting patiently for the perfect wave; three young mothers trying to keep track of their toddlers and carry on a conversation at the same time; a girl practicing cartwheels at the edge of the crashing surf.

Two hours passed in a flash. As Elizabeth trudged back in the direction of her car, she suddenly realized she was tired. After leaving her perch by the driftwood, she must have walked at least two miles up the beach and back again!

The parking lot was on the other side of a sand dune criss-crossed with footpaths. When she reached the dune, Elizabeth turned to whistle for Prince Albert who was happily loping behind her. That was when she saw three men running along the next path.

Elizabeth stared at the men, her attention captivated. There was something odd about them. *They're running too closely together, that's it*, she observed. *And they're not dressed for jogging.* The youngest was wearing jeans and a T-shirt; the other two men, who looked to be in their late thirties, were wearing trousers and sports shirts.

But it was more than that. Somehow, there was a sense of uneasiness surrounding the trio. Whatever it was, they made a striking image. Intrigued, Elizabeth lifted her camera, focused quickly, and snapped a picture.

As she was about to take a second photograph, one of the older men happened to look in her direction. She noticed he was very red in the face and sweat gleamed on his balding forehead. He stopped in his tracks and glared at her. "What do you think you're doing?" he yelled.

"Just taking a picture," Elizabeth replied, stating the obvious. And before Elizabeth could apologize for any unintended offense she might have given, the man was running toward her. The next thing Elizabeth knew, he tried to snatch her camera right out of her hand!

"Hey!" Elizabeth yelled, yanking the camera out of his reach.

Suddenly, Elizabeth heard a menacing snarl. Prince Albert ran up and jumped up on the man, his teeth bared.

The bald man fell back in surprise.

Quickly, Elizabeth sprinted over the dune to her parked car. She jumped inside and started the engine, looking over her shoulder anxiously. The man hadn't given up; he was chasing her!

Prince Albert ran after the man, barking loudly. Elizabeth didn't hesitate. She had to trust her dog to know what to do. She couldn't risk having that man catch up to her!

"Come on, Prince Albert!" Elizabeth shouted, her voice high with fear. Then she hit the gas.

With a bound, Prince Albert overtook the

man and leapt into the back of the convertible just as Elizabeth pulled away.

In the rearview mirror, Elizabeth saw the man stop at the edge of the parking lot and shake his fist after her departing car. The other two men had disappeared from sight.

Elizabeth gripped the steering wheel, her heart pounding, and sped out of the parking lot onto the road. She took a few deep breaths and reminded herself she was all right. *That man must have been crazy*, she thought.

After dinner that night, Todd picked up Elizabeth in the new BMW his parents had given to him when the family had moved back to California. The two stopped at Casey's Ice Cream Parlor in the Valley Mall on their way to Todd's house to do homework together.

They had been sitting in the car in the parking lot for five minutes. Todd was almost finished with his cone but Elizabeth had barely touched hers.

"Something's on your mind, Liz, I can tell," her boyfriend observed. "What could be more important than chocolate chip ice cream?"

Elizabeth smiled. She *was* preoccupied; she couldn't hide it. "I had a strange experience this afternoon, that's all. Make that a *scary* experience." She paused to lick around the edge of her melting cone.

Todd frowned. "What do you mean?"

"I'm all right," Elizabeth hurried to assure him. "I just got spooked. I was at the beach this afternoon, taking pictures with Regina's camera. And I saw these three men running."

Elizabeth hadn't mentioned the incident to her family. She hadn't wanted to upset them. Now, as she told Todd about her encounter with the menacing bald man, she realized it didn't sound as bizarre and frightening as it had seemed while it was happening.

"The guy was definitely a jerk," Todd commented. "But I'm sure he wasn't trying to hurt you. He just didn't want you to take his picture." He grinned. "Sometimes even *I* feel that way!"

Elizabeth handed her ice cream cone to Todd. She couldn't finish it. "It was more than that. He was mad, really mad. He didn't just yell at me for taking the picture. He tried to grab my camera!"

"Maybe you should be more careful about who you take pictures of," Todd suggested. "You have to expect that some people, like this guy obviously, are going to think of it as an invasion of privacy."

Elizabeth shook her head, unconvinced.

33

"Don't take it so seriously. After all, it goes with the territory. There's some danger involved with being a photographer-at-large," Todd teased.

Elizabeth forced a smile. "I guess."

Todd continued to try to kid her out of her pensive mood. "I bet he was a celebrity, a movie star. You know how they hate the *paparazzi*."

"This man was *not* a movie star!" Elizabeth declared with a giggle. "He was bald and totally unglamorous."

"A movie producer, then." Todd had polished off Elizabeth's cone and was ready to start the BMW. It took a few turns of the key before the engine turned over.

"Is there something wrong with the car?" Elizabeth asked as they pulled out of the parking lot.

"I'm beginning to think so. Probably something wrong with the ignition mechanism."

Elizabeth sensed that Todd didn't want to admit that his new car might need repairs so soon.

At the Wilkinses', Elizabeth and Todd settled comfortably on the rec room sofa with their books. Todd plunged right into a set of math problems, but Elizabeth couldn't concentrate on her history reading.

She kept hearing Todd's sensible voice in her head. *"He just didn't want you to take his picture."*

But Elizabeth could also hear the bald man's voice. *"Mind your own business."* That was all he'd said, and Elizabeth knew it didn't sound so scary in the retelling. That was because it wasn't the words so much as the bald man's manner that had been threatening. What would he have done if he'd caught her, if Prince Albert hadn't been there to protect her?

Elizabeth shivered. She couldn't study. She couldn't forget how genuinely frightened she had felt that afternoon at the beach. Elizabeth trusted her instincts, and all her instincts told her that Todd was wrong. True, the bald man hadn't wanted Elizabeth to take his picture, but there was more to it.

Still, she had no way of proving that. All she had was a feeling. And a roll of film.

Four

"I never thought the photography club would be so popular that we'd have to take turns using the equipment," said Jim on Wednesday afternoon as he and Elizabeth waited to use an enlarger. Jim beamed like a proud father. "Wonderful, isn't it?"

"Sure is," Elizabeth replied without much enthusiasm. In her opinion, it was anything but wonderful. As a rule, she was a patient person, but today Elizabeth could barely sit still to wait her turn. It seemed as if Allen, Patty, and the others had been monopolizing the enlargers for hours.

Elizabeth had shot and developed two rolls of film since Monday, one of Sweet Valley High faculty for the photo essay and one at the beach on Tuesday. She hoped her pictures of Ms. Dalton and the other teachers had turned out well, but it was the beach pictures she was most interested in. There was one in particular she couldn't wait to see.

Andy Jenkins finished exposing an eight-by-ten print. Elizabeth looked at Jim. "It's all yours," he said. "I can wait a little longer."

Good, Elizabeth thought, hurrying to the enlarger. *Because I can't!*

There were thirty-six pictures on the roll of film, but Elizabeth didn't hesitate over which to print first. Looking through the eyepiece of the enlarger, she centered the negative and the printing paper. First she figured out the correct exposure by doing a test print. Then she proceeded to print the photograph at its correct exposure.

When the correct amount of time had elapsed, Elizabeth flicked off the switch and rushed the print to the row of basins for processing. She immersed it in the first tray that held developer.

Before Elizabeth's eyes, the image of the three men running on the beach slowly emerged. Elizabeth watched carefully, as the details sprang to life. She didn't want the picture to overdevelop. From the basin of developer, she slipped the print into the stop bath and then into the fixer and final water wash. Finally, she was done.

Elizabeth held up the dripping photograph. There they were, in crisp black-and-white: the three men, just as she remembered them.

A chill ran up Elizabeth's spine. The picture brought back the events of that afternoon so clearly. *Too* clearly.

In a way, Elizabeth felt vindicated. The photograph proved that she hadn't just been imagining something strange about the three men.

Elizabeth narrowed her eyes and studied the picture by the orange glow of the safelight. The man in the middle had a pained expression on his face, and the stiff posture of his shoulders made him look distinctly uncomfortable, as if he were being forced to run. And the men on either side of him—the bald man who had attacked Elizabeth and a third man, who was quite young and attractive—seemed to be watching the man in the middle very closely, as if they thought he might try to get away from them.

The photo was like a cryptic message. And Elizabeth wanted to decipher it. She put the picture of the three men in the print dryer, and spent an hour printing some of the other beach shots, as well as a few photographs of her French instructor, Ms. Dalton, and a few of Mr.

Collins, the faculty adviser for *The Oracle* and Elizabeth's favorite teacher at Sweet Valley High.

Finally, she decided to call it a day. She crossed the darkroom to the adjoining room where the student photographers stored their film and pictures in cubbies along one wall.

Elizabeth kept two folders in her cubby, one for prints and one for negatives. She slid the last negative she had printed into its protective plastic sleeve. Then she shuffled through the prints one more time, keeping the Sweet Valley High faculty photos separate from the beach series. There was the old man with the metal detector, the lone surfer, the young mothers— and the three men.

As Elizabeth examined the photograph yet again, the distressing feeling she had experienced returned. But she still couldn't explain just why the picture disturbed and intrigued her so much.

I don't know who these men are, she told herself reasonably. *I don't know what they're doing or why, and I'll probably never know.*

But Elizabeth just couldn't put it out of her mind. She hesitated for a moment, then she put all but one of the prints into her cubby. The photo of the three running men, she slipped into her purse. Before turning away, she reopened the folder holding her negatives. She located the strip containing the shot of the three men and put that in her purse, too.

"Nicholas is getting jealous," Jim heard Andrea tell Claire as they worked in the dark-room. "He looked in the folder I keep my pictures in, and there were about a dozen pictures of Max Dellon. You know, I decided to photograph Sweet Valley High musicians for the mural."

"Who's Max Dellon?" asked Claire.

"The lead guitarist for this rock band called The Droids. They seem to be pretty popular around here," explained Andrea. "And Max is pretty cute. So now Nicholas thinks I have the hots for Max! I was trapped. I couldn't give away the photo-essay project, and I couldn't think of another reason why I'd be following this guy and taking pictures of him!"

Claire laughed. "It's lucky I don't have a boy-friend. My pictures are of the football team!"

Jim saw that Elizabeth was getting ready to leave. "Can you stick around a little longer?" he asked her.

"Sure," she said. "What's going on?"

"A bunch of people have already gone home, but I thought before we lock up, the rest of us could take a look at what we have so far for the photo essay."

A few minutes later Jim, Elizabeth, Claire, Andrea, DeeDee, Patty, Andy, and Tina had spread out their photographs on the big table in the room next door. Jim and Tina were working in both color and black-and-white; the less-experienced photographers were sticking to black-and-white.

Jim was full of enthusiasm. It was pretty exciting to see everybody's pictures and start imagining what the finished project would look like. "We can pretend the tabletop is part of the wall space in the main lobby we'll be using for the photo essay," he suggested.

"I'm going to have a lot more than this." Elizabeth put an eight-by-ten of Mr. Collins next to one of Ms. Dalton. Underneath them, she arranged five-by-sevens of science instructor Mr. Russo and of Mr. Fellows, who taught history, along with a few group shots she'd taken by sneaking into the faculty lounge.

"Most of us probably will," Jim replied. "That's OK. We can fill the entire wall if we want."

At that moment, the door to the classroom sprang open. Everyone looked up, and Jim jumped to his feet, trying to block part of the table with his body.

It was Jessica, wearing her Sweet Valley High cheerleading jacket. She was obviously annoyed. "Here you are, Liz!" Jessica exclaimed. "I need the car keys, *now*. And this time, not just to go shopping. Mom wanted me to—"

Jessica finally noticed how the photography-club members had reacted to her arrival. They were all standing with their arms held out, trying to hide the table behind them. "Hey, what's going on in here?" Jessica asked, her eyes widening with curiosity. She stepped forward.

Elizabeth quickly intercepted her sister, wheeled her around, and pushed her toward the door. "Here," she said, pulling a set of keys from her purse and tossing them to Jessica. " 'Bye!"

"But—"

Jessica didn't get a chance to finish her sentence. Elizabeth shut the door in her face.

"Sorry about that," Elizabeth apologized to the others.

"Don't worry about it. It's not the first close call we've had." Jim laughed. "And it won't be the last!"

His prediction came true a few minutes later when the door bounced open again. This time it was Shelley, her hair damp from a shower, a big smile on her face.

42

"Are you about done?" she asked brightly. "If not, I'll just hang around here with—"

"No, you won't!" Following Elizabeth's example, Jim dashed to Shelley's side and propelled her through the door and into the hallway before she had a chance to see what was displayed on the table.

"What are you doing?" she cried, her eyes flashing with indignation.

"Sorry, Shelley." He smiled sheepishly. "But it's a secret."

"I swear, you'd think this was the Pentagon and you had blueprints for the Stealth Bomber in there!"

"One of these days—"

"I know, I know. One of these days I'll get to find out what it's all about. Well, I'm not holding my breath!"

"I'll call you tonight," he promised, shutting the door between them.

Rubbing his forehead, Jim returned to the table. He had a feeling he had really ticked Shelley off this time. It was the first time since they began dating that he had kept anything from her. But he knew it was for a good cause. Sweet Valley High, and Shelley, wouldn't have to wait too much longer to discover the photography club's secret.

*   *   *

"Maybe they're performing some kind of satanic voodoo rituals," Lila suggested when Jessica told her about barging in on the photography club meeting the day before. It was Thursday afternoon, and the two girls were driving to the beach in the Fiat. "Maybe they take pictures of people and then stick pins in them."

Jessica knew her friend meant that as a joke. But the photography club was definitely up to something. "Hmmm." Jessica frowned. "Liz kicked me out of there pretty fast. They sure are a weird bunch. That drip Allen Walters, sneaking pictures of the cheerleaders the other day when we were practicing our pyramid. Hey!" A crazy thought struck Jessica. "Maybe he's going to jinx us! Fix it so that every time we try the pyramid, we fall down!"

"Jessica, I was just kidding," said Lila. "Get a grip on yourself. Who cares about the dumb photography club anyway?"

"You're right." Jessica raised a hand to adjust the rearview mirror. "Liz can do whatever she wants with her camera. I finally got the car away from her, two days in a row now. That's all that matters to me."

Lila pushed a strand of windblown hair away

44

from her face. "Me, too. That and getting to the beach before the sun sets. Can't you drive a little faster?"

"I'm sorry, but I don't have a father who can arrange to have my speeding tickets fixed like *some* people I know," Jessica reminded her wealthy friend. "I have a father who'll ground me for life if I get caught speeding."

Jessica braked at a stoplight, then made a right turn, aware of a car close behind her. A mile later, she glanced in the rearview mirror, scowled, and tapped her brakes. The light blue convertible behind the Fiat didn't seem to get the message. It was still tailgating her.

Tailgating—or following her? Jessica made two more turns, and the car stayed close behind her. "Hey, Li," she said grimly. "Don't look now, but I think we're being followed."

Of course Lila looked; Jessica knew she would. Turning all the way around in her seat, Lila lowered her sunglasses and stared blatantly at the driver of the other car. "He's pretty cute, Jess."

From the rearview mirror, Jessica couldn't really see the guy. About all she could tell was that he had blond hair. But out of the corner of her eye she *could* see the smile Lila was flashing at him. "How cute?"

45

"Extremely cute," Lila gushed. "Maybe you should pull over. I'm serious."

If Lila said the driver of the light blue convertible was extremely cute, then he *was* extremely cute. Jessica and Lila clashed on a regular basis, but there was one thing they always agreed on: good-looking guys. Jessica pulled over.

Sure enough, the other car pulled over, too. Jessica heard a car door slam. "Here he comes!" Lila whispered. "Wow, is he gorgeous."

"Wow" was right. The boy walking toward the Fiat took Jessica's breath away. *What a body*, she thought, admiring the way his T-shirt fit a little snugly, making the most of his broad chest and muscular arms. His longish blond hair was almost white in the sun, and the eyes that were glued to Jessica's face were sky-blue. Jessica felt herself melting against the seat.

"So, it *is* you," the guy said, bending over to rest his arms on the car door. "I'm glad you pulled over."

His face was close to Jessica's. She could see that he was a little older than she and Lila were, maybe nineteen or twenty. And those eyes. They were absolutely riveting. *I'm glad I pulled over, too!* Jessica thought.

"I just wanted to apologize," the gorgeous boy continued. He gave her a disarming smile.

"For what happened at the beach a couple of days ago."

Jessica went blank, but only for an instant. Of course. He'd mistaken her for her twin. It happened all the time.

But what was he talking about? What had happened at the beach? Jessica glanced at Lila, who raised her eyebrows, clearly mystified. "Oh, well, that's OK," Jessica said with a shrug. "It was nothing."

"I'm afraid my friend has a problem with his temper," the boy explained. "But he really didn't mean any harm."

"Apology accepted," Jessica assured him, although she still had no idea what he was apologizing for. He and Elizabeth must have had a brief encounter at the beach. Whatever the circumstances, Elizabeth obviously hadn't capitalized on the opportunity, probably because she already had a boyfriend and she was unutterably loyal and dull. *Lucky thing I'm not tied down like that!* Jessica thought.

"By the way, my name's Chad."

The two girls introduced themselves. Chad gave Lila's hand a brief shake. Then he took Jessica's hand and held it for a significantly long moment. Chad was practically ignoring Lila, and Jessica loved it. His gaze hadn't left

47

her face for a second. No doubt about it, he was flirting with her.

"By the way, you wouldn't happen to have a copy of that picture, would you?" Chad asked suddenly.

Jessica blinked. "Picture?"

Suddenly the situation started to make some sense. Regina Morrow's camera and the stupid photography club! Elizabeth must have gone to the beach earlier that week and taken a picture of Chad and his friend, the one Chad said had such a bad temper. Well, Jessica certainly couldn't fault Elizabeth's artistic taste. Chad had to be about as photogenic as they came.

"Um . . ." She had to come up with something to keep this guy talking a little longer! "We just developed it," Jessica fibbed. "Didn't we, Lila?"

"Oh, sure," Lila said. "It turned out really well."

"Great." Chad smiled. "Do you have it with you? I'd sure like to see it."

The second fib always came easier to Jessica than the first. "No, it's at school."

"School?"

"Sweet Valley High," Jessica elaborated. "I left the picture in the darkroom." Jessica tried to recall some of the photography terms she had heard Elizabeth use. "Uh, it's drying."

48

Chad didn't seem to suspect that Jessica didn't know what she was talking about. "Well, maybe when it's dry, you'll let me see it."

Chad had just offered the perfect excuse to keep in touch and Jessica jumped at it. "In order to see the picture, you'll have to see me." She gave Chad an inviting smile.

"Sounds fine to me," he said. "Why don't you give me your phone number?"

Jessica was more than happy to satisfy his request. Taking a scrap of paper and a pen from the glove compartment, she wrote out her phone number. As she passed it to Chad, their hands touched again. An electric tingle brushed up Jessica's arm.

"Call me in a day or two," she said as she turned the key in the ignition.

Chad stepped back from the car. "I'll do that," he promised her.

Jessica pulled back onto the road, a triumphant grin on her face. "You're not going to pout just because he picked me over you, are you, Li?"

"He only picked *you* because he thought you were Liz and she'd already caught his eye somehow or other," Lila replied easily. "Otherwise, you know the Fowler charm would have prevailed."

Jessica laughed. "Whatever you say, Li. It's me he's going to call."

"Yeah, because he wants to see that picture your sister took!"

"No problem. I'll just get it from Liz. She'll be more than happy to further the cause of true love!"

Maybe the photography club is good for something after all! Jessica thought as she continued on toward the beach.

Five

"How about stopping at the Dairi Burger?" Lila suggested a few hours later as she and Jessica tossed their beach towels in the back area of the Fiat. "Napping in the sun always makes me hungry."

"I *could* really go for some fries and a shake," Jessica admitted. "But I should get home. I'm supposed to cook tonight, and I have no idea what I'm going to make." Because Mr. and Mrs. Wakefield both worked, the twins took turns helping out with dinner a few times a week. "Besides, I can't wait to tell Liz about meeting Chad!"

"You mean to tell Liz about *stealing* Chad," Lila corrected her.

"I didn't steal him," Jessica protested. "Liz

had her chance on the beach the other day. You know her. She's so devoted to Todd, she doesn't even look at other guys."

"Obviously she looked at Chad. She took his picture!" Lila said, taking a mirror from her purse and checking her nose for sunburn.

Jessica dropped Lila off at Fowler Crest. Usually, the enormous Spanish-style mansion with its fountain and sculptured grounds, one of the most opulent residences in Sweet Valley, caused Jessica a pang or two of envy. But that day Jessica wouldn't have traded places with Lila for the world. Lila wasn't the one who would be getting a call from Chad!

Jessica coasted up the driveway of her family's split-level house and killed the engine. When she got inside, she sprinted up the stairs.

"Liz, are you up here?" she yelled. Jessica barged into her twin's room without bothering to knock.

Elizabeth was wearing a terry-cloth bathrobe and holding a new bottle of shampoo. The shower was already running in the bathroom that connected the twins' bedrooms. "Hi, Jess," Elizabeth said as she stepped into the bathroom.

"I have the wildest story to tell you!" Jessica announced. "You'll never believe what happened on the way to the beach. Lila and I were

52

just driving along, minding our own business, when—"

Elizabeth shook her head and started to close the bathroom door between them. "I have to jump in the shower. I'm going over to Todd's for dinner, and I'm already running late."

"I'll make it quick," Jessica promised. "So, there we were, just driving along, when I noticed this car was following us. And, Liz, you'll never guess who—"

"I'll guess later!" Elizabeth said as she shut the bathroom door behind her.

"Dinner at Todd's, big deal," Jessica mumbled to herself as she headed down the hall. As usual, her own bedroom was quite a contrast to Elizabeth's. Everything was always in its proper place in Elizabeth's bright, neat room. Jessica's, on the other hand, was a cross between the bargain basement of a department store and a mud-wrestling pit. Jessica had painted the walls chocolate brown, which was where the mud-pit effect came from. The bargain-basement look resulted from the fact that nearly every item of Jessica's fairly extensive wardrobe was scattered about the room, draped over furniture or just piled on the floor.

Elizabeth wouldn't be out of the shower for at least fifteen minutes, and Jessica had to relate her latest romantic adventure to someone or she would burst. She decided to call her friend Amy Sutton. At least Amy would appreciate the Chad story.

Amy appreciated the Chad story so much that Jessica called Cara Walker, her older brother Steven's girlfriend and one of her own closest friends, and shared it with her, too. After determining that Cara was suitably impressed, Jessica hung up the phone and bounced into the hall. Perfect timing. Her sister had just emerged from her bedroom.

Elizabeth was wearing a deep pink sleeveless dress and a strand of pearls. "You look great, Liz. I guess dinner at Todd's is a little fancier now."

"Um-hum," said Elizabeth, hurrying down the stairs, barely listening to her sister.

A car honked in the driveway. Todd's BMW, Jessica guessed. She chased after her sister, who was already opening the front door. "So, like I was saying. The guy in the car turned out to be cute, and I mean cute. His name's Chad, and the whole reason he was following us was because—"

"I should have known this was about a new boy! It always is. I just don't have time to hear about it right now, OK? Tell me tomorrow."

Standing at the door, Jessica crossed her arms and watched her twin hurry down the walk.

"Just forget it!" she shouted after Elizabeth. "So what if it's because of you that I met Chad in the first place."

But Elizabeth couldn't hear her; the BMW was already rolling out of the driveway.

So what if it was the absolute best coincidence of all time, Jessica thought, wandering into the kitchen to decide on a menu for supper. So what if Chad was probably going to turn out to be the man of Jessica's dreams! If Elizabeth didn't have time to listen, well, Jessica would just keep Chad all to herself.

It would serve Elizabeth right, anyway, Jessica decided as she checked out the contents of the refrigerator. Her sister was Little Miss Secrets these days, making such a fuss about the photography club's activities. Now Jessica had her own secret. From now on, if Elizabeth wanted to know what was new in Jessica's life, she would just have to guess.

"That was delicious," Elizabeth raved as she swallowed the last bite of key lime pie.

"It was, wasn't it?" agreed Mrs. Wilkins. "Having a dinner guest is a good excuse to indulge in a sinful dessert."

"Thanks for going to the trouble."

"You're never any trouble," Mrs. Wilkins

assured her. "You know we consider you family, not company."

Under the table, Todd touched Elizabeth's foot with his. She smiled at him. His family's life-style had changed since Mr. Wilkins's big promotion, but the Wilkinses themselves hadn't. They were still warm, wonderful people. At first, Elizabeth had found the big mansion and formal dining room somewhat intimidating, but now she was just as at home there as she had been in their old house.

Elizabeth helped clear the table. Then she poured out two glasses of iced tea, and she and Todd made themselves comfortable on the rec-room sofa. Using the remote control, Todd flicked on the big-screen TV.

"Time for the news." Todd put his arm around Elizabeth. "And now for tonight's top story." Todd lowered his voice in imitation of an anchorman. "What is the secret project the Sweet Valley High photography club has been working on, night and day? Will Elizabeth Wakefield give in to irresistible pressure from her boyfriend and reveal all?"

Elizabeth giggled. "Never! I'll guard the secret with my life."

"You forget that I know your weakness." Todd started to tickle Elizabeth.

"Todd! Stop! Unless you want to be responsible for spilling iced tea on this new leather couch!"

"OK, you win," he conceded. "As always. And here's the top story for real."

Elizabeth looked from Todd to the TV screen. "And now from Washington," the newscaster said. "There has been an unexpected development in the major drug inquiry underway in the Senate. When hearings resumed today, one of the chief witnesses took everyone by surprise by recanting his previous testimony and offering a very different story."

"I heard about this on the radio earlier," Todd told Elizabeth. "Supposedly this guy was going to testify against some major drug dealers."

The newscaster continued. "Ron Hunter was expected to name participants in what is believed to be the most widespread drug operation in the U.S. In today's session, however, Hunter categorically denied having been involved in any illegal activities. His latest testimony casts doubt upon the very existence of the drug ring."

A picture of a man flanked by two security guards flashed on the screen. *The man in the middle* . . . Elizabeth gasped, surprise stealing her breath away. "Todd!" she cried. "It's him!"

"Who?"

"The man at the beach. My photograph. The man in the middle!"

Todd stared at Elizabeth, then at the TV. An instant later, the picture of Ron Hunter was replaced by one relating to another news item.

"You mean the picture of the three men running?"

Elizabeth was fumbling through her purse. "Ron Hunter! He looks just like him. Here!" She handed the photograph to Todd. "See for yourself!"

Todd studied the print. "I didn't get a very close look at the guy on the TV," he said, "but, yeah, I agree. There's a resemblance between the guy in the middle of your photograph and Ron Hunter."

"A *strong* resemblance," Elizabeth declared. "Maybe that was Ron Hunter I saw on the beach!"

"It couldn't have been," Todd pointed out. "You took the picture two days ago. This guy Hunter's been in Washington all week testifying."

"You're right," Elizabeth said. "But still—"

"You know what I think," Todd continued. "The picture of Hunter in Washington reminded you of *this* one because Ron Hunter was also standing between two men."

"It wasn't just the pose," Elizabeth insisted.

58

"Maybe you didn't get a close look at Ron Hunter, but I did." She sighed. There wasn't any point in arguing about it with Todd. It wasn't just what Elizabeth had seen on the TV; it was that feeling again.

"Something doesn't add up," she said quietly. "Or rather, something adds up, but it adds up all wrong!"

"What do you mean?"

"Why did the bald man try to take my camera away? Todd, he might have hurt me. If Prince Albert hadn't growled at him, if my car hadn't been parked nearby . . ." Elizabeth's heart pounded with remembered fear. "I saw something I wasn't supposed to see, and I had the evidence of it on film. Maybe what I wasn't supposed to see was the resemblance between the guy in the middle and Ron Hunter in Washington!"

Todd shook his head in disbelief. "I know what happened to you on the beach really got to you, Liz. It was a pretty strange incident, I'll grant you that. But connecting it to the drug investigation in the Senate? You kind of lose me there. You have to admit it's a little farfetched."

"I know it sounds crazy." Elizabeth felt frustrated. How could she explain this feeling that didn't have anything to do with logic? "Something tells me there *is* a link between the picture

I took and what's going on in Washington. We've got to find those three men again. It could be important."

Todd ran a hand through his dark hair. "If there's a link, it would be important all right," he agreed. "But that's a big 'if.'"

"You have to believe me." Elizabeth gazed earnestly into Todd's eyes.

Todd bent down and brushed Elizabeth's lips with a kiss. "I do believe you. I always believe you," he assured her. "I'll help. We'll look into this together. But where do we start? How are we going to find the men from the beach, and what will we do if we find them?"

Elizabeth gave Todd a hug. "I knew I could count on you!" she exclaimed. "As for where we start, I guess we have to start with the photograph. It's all we have."

Todd and Elizabeth huddled over the photograph and examined it intently. "I feel like Sherlock Holmes and Watson." Todd laughed. "Maybe I should have a pipe and a big magnifying glass."

"A magnifying glass *would* come in handy. Look at this." Elizabeth tapped the photograph, indicating the young blond man on the left. "He's wearing a T-shirt with some kind of lettering on it. It could be a clue! Can you tell what it says?"

Todd held the photograph close to his eyes. "I can't make it out."

Elizabeth squinted, but she couldn't read the lettering on the T-shirt, either. "Maybe if we enlarged the picture we could read it!"

"A definite possibility," Todd conceded.

"We can do it in the darkroom tomorrow after school!"

Todd placed the photograph on the coffee table and wrapped his arms around Elizabeth. "You're really going to allow me into that sacred place?" he teased.

"I need your expert assistance, Dr. Watson. You just have to promise you'll confine your snooping to reading the mystery man's T-shirt."

"Whatever you say, Sherlock!"

Six

"You don't mind if I take the car to Amy's after cheerleading practice this afternoon, do you?" Jessica asked Elizabeth as they drove to school on Friday morning. "She's having a few people over for a cookout."

"I'll catch a ride with Todd," Elizabeth replied. She was about to tell Jessica about enlarging the photo to try to read the blond guy's T-shirt, but she hesitated. It was a pretty convoluted story, and she didn't feel like explaining all about the Washington news report and her photograph of the three men on the beach to Jessica. It was still too complicated and vague. "I've got to do some work for *The Oracle*, and Todd has practice," Elizabeth finished lamely. She rarely lied, and she felt a little guilty.

"Whatever," said Jessica, oblivious of her twin's discomfort. "By the way, did you have a good time at Todd's last night?"

Elizabeth was aware that there was something odd about Jessica's tone of voice. But what? Had Jessica noticed how preoccupied Elizabeth was this morning? "It was fine," Elizabeth answered. "Mrs. Wilkins cooked a pretty elaborate dinner."

"So it was worth getting all dressed up and flying out of the house in such a rush?"

"I guess."

Jessica seemed to be waiting for Elizabeth to say something else, but Elizabeth couldn't imagine what. She glanced at her twin, who was busy polishing the lenses of her sunglasses. "Why do you ask?" Elizabeth pulled into a space in the Sweet Valley High student parking lot.

"Oh, just forget it!" Jessica grabbed her book bag, hopped out of the car, and flounced across the parking lot without waiting for Elizabeth.

Suddenly Elizabeth remembered that the night before Jessica had tried to tell her about a cute new boy she had met. She must have hurt Jessica's feelings by not showing more interest.

Elizabeth caught up with her twin at the front entrance to the school. "Jess, I was meaning to ask you. What's this about—"

63

"Look, Liz—police!" Jessica interrupted. "I wonder what's going on?"

Three Sweet Valley police officers stood in the main lobby, talking to a cluster of high-school administrators, including the principal, "Chrome Dome" Cooper. A group of students stood around them, chattering with excitement. Elizabeth caught the words "vandals" and "darkroom."

She tapped the nearest person on the shoulder. "What happened?" Elizabeth asked the boy. "Why are the police here?"

"There was a break-in last night," the boy explained. "They said that the darkroom was the only part of the school that was vandalized, but supposedly it's pretty trashed."

Jessica saw Lila and Amy on the other side of the lobby and ran over to talk to them, while Elizabeth wandered in the direction of her homeroom. Someone had vandalized the darkroom. Who? And why?

For Elizabeth, the day passed in a blur. With every hour, she grew more and more distracted. Had any harm come to the club's pictures for the photo essay? The instant the final bell rang, she raced through the crowded halls toward the darkroom. She was anxious to see for herself what had happened. At lunch, the

64

darkroom had been off limits while the police conducted their investigation.

When she reached the photography-club room, Elizabeth saw that all of the members, plus the yearbook and *Oracle* photographers, were either in the darkroom or the main room. Their faces registered their shock.

Canisters of film were ripped open and scattered everywhere. Equipment was overturned, and the floor was littered with torn and trampled photographs. Elizabeth bit her lip to keep from crying. All their work was ruined!

"Can I have everybody's attention?" Mr. Marks called. "I've been put in charge of getting this place back together. I know you all stopped in because you're worried about your photos, but after you've gotten your own things in order, I'd appreciate it if you'd stick around and help with the general clean-up. Jim and Allen, would you two help me determine which of the enlargers are going to need to go out for repairs?"

"What happened, Mr. Marks?" asked Tina, stooping to pick up a handful of crumpled black-and-white prints. "Why would somebody break in to the school just to mess up the darkroom and destroy our prints?"

"It beats me," Mr. Marks admitted. "The police looked around pretty carefully, but from what I heard, they didn't come up with any significant leads."

Jim frowned. "Do you think someone was trying to sabotage our photo-essay project?"

"It doesn't seem likely." Mr. Marks gazed around the room, and his eyes came to rest on the row of cubbies where the students stored their photos. "If you ask me, it looks as if the vandals were looking for something in particular. See the way all the folders were emptied out?" Mr. Marks shook his head. "Whatever the motive, it's going to be awhile before everything is in working order again."

Elizabeth crossed the room to the cubbies. Was it her imagination, or did her cubby look as if it had been disturbed more than the others?

The photographs she had taken of Sweet Valley High teachers had been tossed back into the cubby, but the pictures Elizabeth had shot earlier that week at the beach were flung around at random. The plastic sleeves containing her negatives were also torn and scattered.

As she bent to retrieve some of the negatives, a sick feeling grew in the pit of Elizabeth's stomach. Mr. Marks suspected that the vandals had been looking for something in particular, and Elizabeth had a terrible hunch that she knew what that something was.

The photograph, she thought. *The one of the three men on the beach.*

But how had they known to look for it at the Sweet Valley High photography club? How had they tracked her down? A wave of fear washed over Elizabeth. If it really had been the bald man and his friends who had broken in to search for her photograph, then they knew who she was. They knew where to find her.

Was it because of me that all this damage was done? Elizabeth thought, looking around the room with remorse. Of course she couldn't know for certain. But there was one thing Elizabeth was sure of. If the vandals were looking for her picture of the Ron Hunter look-alike and the other two men, then they had gone away unsatisfied. She had been carrying the print and the negative in her purse all along.

Elizabeth returned the crumpled beach pictures to her cubby. Realizing that her hands were shaking, she squeezed them into fists. The feeling was stronger than ever. There was something wrong, terribly wrong. And she was sure that the picture of the three men on the beach was the key.

And now that the darkroom was out of service, she wouldn't be able to use it to enlarge the photograph and read the lettering on the blond man's T-shirt. She and Todd would just have to find another way, because finding out about the three mysterious men on the beach was now more urgent than ever.

When Jim had asked Shelley at lunch if they would be meeting as usual that afternoon, she had gotten a little huffy. "I'm always done with basketball first, and I'm sick of stopping by the darkroom and being treated like some kind of spy!" she had declared.

"Then let's meet at the Dairi Burger later," he had suggested. "Around four-thirty. That should give me enough time to check out the darkroom situation. Is it a date?"

"Sure. It's a date," Shelley had agreed. She couldn't stay angry at her boyfriend for long.

But now, Shelley and the Dairi Burger were the farthest things from Jim's mind. He couldn't believe what chaos the darkroom was in. It was even worse than he'd expected. And it seemed such mindless destruction. Why would anybody do such a thing?

After an hour of cleaning, there was still a long way to go. It was very discouraging. Several of the enlargers were damaged beyond saving, and there wasn't a single one that didn't need repair. And in addition to prints and negatives being spoiled, many rolls of film that had not been developed yet were ruined, ripped right out of the canisters. *Pictures we'll never see*, Jim thought sadly.

It really broke his heart. He felt very protective toward the club. After all, the whole thing was his idea in the first place. And now, it looked like a disaster area. Jim kicked at an empty film canister. "What are we going to do about our photo essay?" he asked.

Allen shook his head glumly. "We were supposed to be putting it all together a week from now."

"We're going to have to start from scratch!" wailed Tina.

"Maybe not," Mr. Marks said, trying to be encouraging. "There may be a lot of stuff here we can salvage. If not prints, at least some of the negatives. Before we panic, let's take a look."

Jim and the other photography-club members spread the rumpled prints and strips of negatives on the table.

"Mr. Marks is right. Maybe it's not so bad." Claire held up a few strips of negatives in plastic sleeves. "These are fine. Who took pictures of the tennis team?"

"Those are mine," said John Pfeifer. "Thanks."

"And that's what's important," Jim pointed out, his optimism reviving. "It doesn't matter so much if people's prints got messed up, as long as the negatives are OK. We can make new prints from them."

Patty held up a strip of negatives and frowned. "What if there's a scratch in one? Does that mean it's wrecked? This was one of my favorite pictures."

"A scratch in a negative will make a white line across the print," answered Jim. "But there's a technique that sometimes works. I'll show you how as soon as the darkroom's back in order."

The time flew by as they worked. Jim didn't even think to check his watch until five-thirty, and then he remembered: Shelley. He was supposed to have met her at the Dairi Burger an hour ago!

Jim stowed the negatives and prints he had recovered and rushed out to the student parking lot. He pulled out of the lot, tires squealing. He knew Shelley would be mad, but Jim was sure she would understand when he explained how bad the darkroom situation had turned out to be.

Jim spotted Shelley as soon as he pulled into the Dairi Burger parking lot. She was just leaving the popular Sweet Valley hangout with Greg Hilliard, a star on the boys' basketball team and Shelley's neighbor and friend since childhood.

Jim jumped out of his car and hurried to Shelley, who was about to climb into Greg's Jeep. "Hey, Shelley!" Jim called. "You're not leaving, are you?"

"You bet I'm leaving. I've been hanging around here for hours!"

"I'm really sorry," Jim said sincerely. "But the darkroom was a mess, and the club had to—"

Shelley cut him off. "Don't tell me. I'm sure it's top-secret information and you'll be sorry you gave in and revealed it in a moment of weakness."

Greg laughed and Jim frowned. "I've told you that I'll explain it all soon. Actually, it will explain itself."

Shelley tossed her head. "I'm really not interested in an explanation. I really couldn't care less!"

"Please, Shel," Jim cajoled, putting a hand on her arm. "Let's talk. I'll buy you a milkshake."

"Greg already bought me one." Shelley climbed into the passenger seat of the Jeep. "And now we're off to shoot some hoops."

Jim looked at Greg, who lifted his hands

71

helplessly. "Well, I'll call you later," Jim promised Shelley.

Shelley didn't reply.

"So long, Roberts," said Greg as he started the Jeep's engine.

Jim stared after the Jeep until it was out of sight. Then he shook himself. For a moment, he considered grabbing a burger and a shake. Instead, he returned to his car. He didn't really have much of an appetite.

Jim supposed he couldn't blame Shelley for being disappointed and angry. He was never happy with himself for letting her down in even the smallest way. But she didn't have to make such a big deal just now. Stomping off with another guy, and Greg Hilliard, of all people. Jim knew that Shelley had had a crush on Greg for a long time before she and Jim became a couple. But Shelley's being with Greg didn't mean anything, did it? Jim realized now that in some ways, he still didn't know Shelley.

What a lousy day, Jim thought morosely as he pointed his car toward home. The darkroom had gotten vandalized, and suddenly his relationship with Shelley seemed to be in jeopardy, too.

Seven

Elizabeth finished loading her family's Saturday-morning breakfast dishes in the dishwasher. Then she dialed Todd's phone number.

"Hi, it's me," she said when he picked up the phone.

"So, what's the game plan?"

Holding the phone between her ear and shoulder, Elizabeth hoisted herself up onto the kitchen counter. "I mentioned to Jessica that I needed to find someplace to work since I can't use the darkroom at school. She reminded me that Amy Sutton's father is a free-lance photographer. He has a studio right downtown."

Elizabeth knew Amy's parents well. When

they were children, Elizabeth and Amy were best friends; now, Amy was more Jessica's friend than Elizabeth's.

"That's great!" exclaimed Todd. "Are you going to give him a call?"

"I just did," Elizabeth replied. "About half an hour ago. Mr. Sutton was really nice. He's not working today, though. But he said he'd love to help us out. We can come by on Monday after school and use his darkroom."

"Can you wait until then?" Todd asked.

Elizabeth didn't really want to. Since the break-in at the Sweet Valley High darkroom, her curiosity was stronger than ever. She couldn't help but feel that there was no time to waste, but they didn't seem to have a choice. In fact, after calling Mr. Sutton, Elizabeth had called all of the commercial darkrooms in the area in the hope that one would be open on the weekend. None were.

"We don't have much of a choice, do we?" she said. "I'll just have to settle for reading the newspapers and watching the news on TV to see if I can find out anything significant about Ron Hunter and the drug hearing in Washington!"

Todd laughed. "Let me know if you do. We're still going to Secca Lake today, though, aren't we? I'll pick you up around noon."

"OK. 'Bye."

Elizabeth hung up the phone. Before she had a chance to hop down from the counter, it rang again.

"Hello, I'd like to speak to Jessica," a male voice announced.

"She's not here," Elizabeth answered. "Can I take a message?"

"When will she be back?" the caller asked bluntly.

"I don't really know." At ten, about the time she was phoning Mr. Sutton, Elizabeth had seen her twin dash out of the house, but she had no idea where Jessica was going or when she'd be back. All she knew was that it was unusual for Jessica to be up, let alone leaving the house, that early on a Saturday morning. "I'm not sure if she went out for the whole day or just on an errand. If you give me your phone number—"

"No. I'll try her later. Tell her Chad called."

Elizabeth couldn't say much for Jessica's latest admirer's phone manners, but she made an effort to be polite. "I'll tell her. Chad . . ."

Elizabeth paused, expecting Chad to fill in the blank with his last name. He hung up on her instead.

Shaking her head, Elizabeth replaced the

receiver. She didn't know where Jessica found some of the guys she dated. This one sounded like a real jerk.

Elizabeth crossed the kitchen on her way to the hallway and the stairs. At that moment, Jessica burst into the kitchen. "Amy and I got all the way to Lila's before I realized I'd left the goop in the fridge!"

Elizabeth watched as her sister removed a covered mixing bowl from the refrigerator. "Goop?"

"For our hair," Jessica explained. "Amy found the recipe in a magazine. It's going to give us great highlights."

Elizabeth wrinkled her nose. She was familiar with the nutty beauty treatments Jessica and her friends experimented with. "I'm afraid to ask, but I will anyway. What's in it?"

"Mayonnaise, lemon juice, mashed avocado, and beer. Don't worry," Jessica assured Elizabeth. "Dad gave me permission to use the beer any way I wanted as long as I didn't drink it!"

"Ugh. Better you than me!"

Bowl in hand, Jessica started to head back out. "Hold on, Jess," Elizabeth called after her. "Before I forget, I just took a call for you."

"Yeah? From who?"

"A guy named Chad."

Jessica gave an excited hop. "Really? What did he say?"

"Not much," Elizabeth replied. "He sounded pretty eager to talk to you, though."

"Did he leave his number?"

"No. He said he'd call back."

"Do me a favor," said Jessica. "If Chad calls again while I'm at Lila's, give him her phone number, OK?"

"Will do," Elizabeth promised. "So, who is this guy, anyway?"

Jessica lifted her chin. "I'm sure you don't have time to hear about a trivial thing like my love life," she said airily. "Don't you have some film you need to develop or a dinner party to attend?"

Elizabeth laughed. "Spill the beans. I have time now, really."

"Well, I don't!" Turning on her heel, Jessica breezed out of the kitchen. "Ta-ta, Liz!"

Heading upstairs to put on her bathing suit, Elizabeth thought briefly about this mysterious Chad. She knew her twin would relent and give her the whole scoop one of these days. For Jessica, half the fun of meeting a wonderful guy was talking about him.

When she got to her bedroom, Elizabeth took the photograph of the three men on the beach out of her purse. If only she could read the lettering on the blond man's T-shirt! If only Monday wasn't two whole days away!

The instant the final bell rang on Monday, Elizabeth sprinted for Todd's locker. "Come on!" she cried, grabbing her boyfriend's arm. "Let's beat the rush leaving the parking lot."

"Whoa! Can't I even get the books I need for my homework tonight?"

"Nope."

"But, Liz—"

"I'm kidding about the books," she told him and smiled. "But I'm not kidding about being in a hurry!"

Todd grinned. "All right. I'm ready. Lead the way!"

Tugging Todd's hand, Elizabeth led him to the car. Todd put the key in the ignition and turned it. Nothing happened.

"Don't do this to me," he said under his breath. He turned the key again. Still nothing.

"Quit kidding around!" Elizabeth begged.

"I'm not kidding," Todd protested. "It won't start."

Elizabeth wanted to scream. She had had to wait all weekend to go to Mr. Sutton's darkroom and enlarge the photograph. Now it looked as if she might not get there today, either.

She bounced impatiently in her seat. "Why won't it start? Can't you do something?"

"I'm trying! I think there's something wrong with one of the ignition coils. I usually manage to get it going eventually. I guess I'll have to take it back to the dealership for some work. At least it's still under warranty."

Just as Elizabeth thought she would explode, Todd turned the key one more time, and the engine rumbled slowly into life. Todd gave her the thumbs-up sign. "Here we go!"

It was just as well Todd was driving, Elizabeth thought as they headed downtown. She would have had a hard time staying within the speed limit.

Todd parked the BMW on Main Street in front of Mr. Sutton's photography studio. The two hurried inside.

Mr. Sutton, who was working at a light table, looked up as Elizabeth and Todd entered. "Hi there, Liz. Nice to see you again!"

"Hello, Mr. Sutton. Do you know Todd Wilkins?"

Mr. Sutton shook Todd's hand. "Of course. Everyone knows the star of the Sweet Valley High basketball team!"

"Thanks for letting us come by," Elizabeth

said. "I hope this isn't an inconvenience for you."

"Not at all," Mr. Sutton assured her. "The darkroom's all yours. Help yourself to anything and everything and just give a holler if you need help."

From Elizabeth's point of view, the arrangement was perfect. She had hoped to get away without showing the photograph of the three men to Mr. Sutton, and it appeared that he wasn't going to ask any questions about her urgent project.

"What should I do?" Todd asked Elizabeth as she prepared to make the enlargement.

"Just cross your fingers."

Focusing the enlarger, she zeroed in on the three men. Then she exposed the eight-by-ten print, timing it by the second hand on her watch.

She and Todd both held their breath as the print developed. "It's done," Elizabeth announced. "Now for the stop bath, and the fixer, and the rinse." After that was finished, she lifted the print from the last basin. "Let's take a look!"

Together they peered at the still-wet photograph. The lettering on the T-shirt was clearer, but still not clear enough. "I can't read it," Todd confessed.

"Me neither," said Elizabeth, overcome with a wave of disappointment.

Todd put an arm around her shoulders. "Hey, don't give up. You said it to me in the car just now—keep trying."

"You're right!" Elizabeth gave Todd a quick kiss. "If I can get the T-shirt a little bigger, I'm sure we'll be able to make out what it says."

Once again, she focused carefully. She was making another eight-by-ten, but this time the figure of the blond man in the T-shirt took up the entire print. "This has to do it!" Elizabeth said hopefully as she slipped the exposed paper into the developer.

This time, her disappointment was so intense it almost hurt. "It's still not clear enough."

Todd shook his head. "I think you've done all you can, Liz."

Elizabeth clutched the print, straining her eyes as hard as she could. Why did the lettering on the T-shirt have to be so elusive?

"And even if we could read it," Todd continued, "what's the chance the lettering would even mean anything to us?"

The chance was slim, Elizabeth knew that, but it was there. "I'm going to try one more time. At the maximum enlargement."

"Go for it!" Todd cheered.

It has to work, it has to work, Elizabeth told

herself. She centered the variable focus lens on the T-shirt and twisted the knob that raised and lowered the enlarger. The chant went on in Elizabeth's brain as she timed the exposure. *It has to work, it has to work. . . .*

Elizabeth immersed the exposed paper in the developer. They waited. Slowly, the photograph darkened, sharpened. The lettering on the T-shirt sprang to life. It was legible!

Elizabeth rushed the print to the stop bath. "It worked!" she cried. "Just barely, but look!"

Todd gazed over Elizabeth's shoulder. He squinted, then read, " 'Rick's Place'. That's what it says. 'Rick's Place'," he repeated. "Does that ring a bell with you?"

"No," admitted Elizabeth.

"It's not much to go on."

"But it's a start!" Elizabeth declared, her eyes sparkling with excitement.

As soon as she had finished processing the print, Elizabeth scooped up the still-wet photos. "Come on!"

"Now where are you dragging me?"

"To the nearest telephone book."

In the outer office, Elizabeth and Todd thanked Mr. Sutton and said goodbye. "He probably had a phone book," Todd pointed out as they stepped onto the sidewalk.

"I know, but I really want to keep this to ourselves. There's a pay phone across the street!"

A fat Yellow Pages was chained inside the phone booth. "What do you think?" Elizabeth asked as she riffled quickly through the volume. "A store? A bar or restaurant?"

"Look under restaurants," Todd suggested. "Rick's Place sounds like it would be a bar."

Elizabeth turned to the restaurant section. *N, O, P, Q, R* . . . She stared at the page. "You were right!" Elizabeth was breathless with excitement. "Rick's Place. Here it is!"

Todd scanned the Yellow Pages advertisement. "It's a restaurant in Big Mesa."

Elizabeth took a pen from her purse and quickly jotted the address of Rick's Place on a page corner she tore out of the phone book.

"I hope the food's good," she told Todd. "Because we're going to Rick's Place for dinner tonight!"

"Do you think we'll find out anything there?"

"Probably not," Elizabeth conceded. "I suppose it's a long shot that the blond guy or either of the other men from the beach will be there. But it's worth a try!"

Eight

Jessica got home from cheerleading practice that afternoon at five-thirty. The Wakefield house was quiet. Prince Albert was the only one around to greet her.

And Mom and Dad won't be home until late, Jessica remembered, seeing the note on the refrigerator. Mr. Wakefield was an attorney, and they were having dinner with a client of his. *Boring, boring, boring*, Jessica thought as she grabbed a can of soda from the refrigerator and a bag of chips from the cupboard and started out to sit by the pool in the late-afternoon sun.

The phone rang, stopping her in her tracks. Jessica backed up. "Hello," she said, her mouth full of potato chips.

"Is this Jessica?"

Jessica's heart did a back handspring, and she almost swallowed the chips whole. She recognized that sexy voice. "This is Jessica."

"Jessica, it's Chad."

"Chad!" Jessica exclaimed. Then she calmed herself and tried to sound cool. "I got the message that you called a couple of days ago. I was wondering if I'd hear from you again."

"You're hearing from me," he said with a husky laugh. "I've been kind of busy, but I didn't plan to let you get away."

This was exactly what Jessica wanted to hear. When Chad hadn't called back on Saturday or on Sunday, she had been more than a little worried that he had lost interest.

"Jessica, I want to see you."

Chad was so direct, so intense. Jessica felt tingly with anticipation. "You do?"

"Yeah. How about tonight? I really hope you're free."

Jessica was excited by Chad's eagerness. "As a matter of fact, I am."

"Then I'll pick you up at seven."

"Sounds great. See you then!"

She was about to hang up the phone when Chad spoke again. "By the way, Jessica," he added. "Don't forget to bring that picture you took of my friends and me, OK? I'm psyched to see it."

"Oh, right." Jessica bit her lip. She had been so wrapped up in the prospect of seeing Chad again that she had completely forgotten about the element that had brought them together in the first place—Elizabeth's photograph. "Sure," Jessica told Chad. "I'll bring it."

That dumb picture. Why did I have to be so stubborn? Jessica asked herself as she hung up the phone. If she had just told her sister about Chad, Elizabeth would have given her the picture. Jessica checked the clock on the oven. She had no idea where the picture was, but she had an hour and a half to find it.

Jessica paused for a moment in the doorway of Elizabeth's bedroom. But she quickly overcame her conscience and stampeded in, ready to search. She would start with the table Elizabeth used as a desk.

Elizabeth had stacked things neatly on the table: letters, homework assignments, recent issues of *The Oracle*. Jessica shuffled through these papers, scattering them on the floor in the process. No photograph there. Recently Elizabeth had put a file cabinet under the table. Jessica sorted through the drawers. Still no photograph.

Not bothering to close the drawers, Jessica crossed to Elizabeth's night table and yanked open the drawer. "Bingo!" she cried as she spotted a whole pile of black-and-white photographs.

Sitting on the edge of her twin's bed, Jessica flipped through the pictures. Then, with a disappointed groan, she tossed them back in the drawer. They were all of Todd, every last one!

There was a photograph tucked in the edge of the mirror over Elizabeth's dresser, but of course that too was of Todd. Jessica dumped out Elizabeth's jewelry box. No pictures in there. It didn't seem likely that Elizabeth would store photography-club stuff with her clothing, but Jessica figured it was worth a try.

Jessica worked her way down Elizabeth's dresser, disarranging the neat piles of underwear, nightgowns, T-shirts, sweaters, and shorts. Next she ransacked the bookshelves and the closet.

"It's just not here!" Jessica concluded in frustration. She flung herself on Elizabeth's bed. Then she had a funny, desperate thought. Jessica pulled back the bedspread and tossed the pillows onto the floor. She giggled. No, Elizabeth wasn't sleeping with the picture of Chad under her pillow!

Jessica lay back on the bed and stared at the ceiling. She had turned her sister's room upside down. The photograph definitely wasn't there. *Maybe she didn't even develop it yet*, Jessica speculated unhappily. After all, Elizabeth hadn't been able to use the darkroom at school since it had been vandalized.

Jessica sat up and looked around. Elizabeth's room looked as if a cyclone had torn through it. Actually, it looked like her own room!

I could clean it up—or I could start getting ready for my date. It wasn't a hard decision. Chad would be arriving in just an hour. Jessica headed for the shower. She would leave a note apologizing for the mess. This was going to be the date of her life. Elizabeth would understand. She always did.

Forty-five minutes later, Jessica was ransacking her own closet. She had already tried on three different outfits, and none of them had seemed quite right. Chad was a little bit older so she wanted to look more sophisticated. But not too dressed-up. Chad struck her as the casual type. Something sexy and fun . . .

Jessica finally got it right with a silk tank top and a miniskirt. She pirouetted in front of the full-length mirror and admired her reflection. Now for some jewelry and makeup.

Jessica was in the bathroom dabbing mascara on her eyelashes when the door bell rang. Chad was here already! Jessica flew back into her bedroom and stuck her feet into a pair of flats, then grabbed her purse and her Sweet Valley

High cheerleading jacket. As she walked down the hall to the stairs, she thought of Elizabeth's room and the mess she had left it in. She had meant to write a note. Well, she didn't have time now. Chad pressed the door bell again.

Jessica hurried downstairs and opened the front door. Chad looked down at her, his light blue eyes glinting and a sexy half-smile on his lips. "Ready to go?" he asked.

Jessica stepped outside. Was she ever!

"I just want to change into long pants," Elizabeth told Todd as he parked the BMW in the Wakefields' driveway. "Then we can go on to Rick's Place, OK?"

"The sooner the better. Even if we don't solve the mystery of the three men on the beach, we can get something to eat. I'm starved!"

They reached the front door. "Poor baby," Elizabeth teased, feeling around in her purse for her house key. "All this sleuthing really takes it out of you, huh?"

"It's open," Todd commented as he turned the knob and gave the door a push.

"Jessica must be home then. I know my parents were going out straight from work." Elizabeth hung her purse over the banister and shouted up the stairs. "Hey, Jess!" There was no answer. "Jessica!" Elizabeth called again. Silence.

"That's funny," Elizabeth remarked. "She's not here. But the door wasn't locked." Suddenly the back of her neck prickled. "Todd, you don't think someone—"

"I think someone just forgot to lock it," he interjected, nipping Elizabeth's suspicion in the bud. "Probably Jessica. She's always forgetting to lock it."

"Not always." But Elizabeth knew Todd was probably right.

She took a deep breath and tried to shake off the irrational whisper of fear. She had been a little jumpy ever since that afternoon at the beach when she took the photograph. "I'll only be a minute," she said as she went upstairs.

"Take your time. I'll wait down here."

By the time she got to the top of the stairs, Elizabeth was laughing at herself for being so ridiculous. Just because the front door was unlocked, she was ready to think the worst! *Todd thinks I'm paranoid, and he's probably right.*

The door to her bedroom was ajar. Elizabeth nudged it all the way open.

She blinked. Was her paranoia making her see things? Clothes pulled out of the dresser drawers, pillows tossed about, her desk and closet in total disarray . . .

Elizabeth clutched the door. Her knees were weak. She tried to call Todd's name, but no sound came out. *They were here*, she thought, terrified. *I'm not imagining this. It's happening.*

For a moment, Elizabeth couldn't move. Then she unfroze and ran back down the stairs.

"Liz, what's the matter?" Todd asked when he saw her pale face and wide, startled eyes.

"My room," Elizabeth gasped. "It's been ransacked! It was the men from the beach, I just know it!"

"Hold on. Take it easy." Todd put his hands on her shoulders. "What do you mean, ransacked?"

"I mean ransacked!" Elizabeth cried. "Come see for yourself!"

"OK, let's check it out." Todd's tone was soothing and sensible. He held his arm around Elizabeth as they walked up the stairs together. With Todd close to her, Elizabeth felt safer. But even so, her heart wouldn't slow down.

"It's a mess," Todd had to admit after taking a look around Elizabeth's bedroom. "But, Liz, I don't think anybody broke into your house. Why would they ransack your room? I was just in the living room where there are a lot more valuables, and nothing in there was touched."

"Because they were looking for something of mine."

"Maybe it was Jessica, looking for something to wear," Todd suggested. "Maybe she had a date tonight."

"But why would she have gone through my file drawers and bookshelves?" Elizabeth countered.

Todd shrugged. "I don't know."

Elizabeth went over to her night table. Her pictures of Todd had obviously interested the intruder. Some of them had been thrown back in the drawer while others had been dropped on the floor.

"It's just like what happened to the darkroom at school," Elizabeth said with quiet conviction. "They were here, or one of them was, anyway. The men from the beach, trying to find the photograph. When they didn't find it in the darkroom, they tracked me home somehow." It was an awful thought. She hadn't found them yet, but they had found her! Elizabeth crossed her arms, hugging herself to keep from shaking.

Todd considered Elizabeth's theory. "I don't know, Liz. To tell you the truth, I still think you're overreacting. But if you really think somebody broke into the house, we should call the police."

Elizabeth scooped up the spilled jewelry from the top of the dresser and returned it to her jewelry box. "I don't think anything was stolen.

No, let's not call the police. Let's just go ahead with our plan.''

"To check out Rick's Place?"

Elizabeth nodded. "It's just this feeling I've had from the start. I know this is all connected somehow to the photograph. But you're right. A feeling isn't enough to go on. That's why we've got to find those men!"

Nine

"So, tell me all about yourself, Jessica," Chad said as he hit the gas to pass a car on Route One.

Jessica pushed a strand of windblown hair out of her eyes and glanced with uncertainty at Chad, who was lighting up another cigarette. It was a perfectly normal first-date question. It was just the *way* Chad asked it. He didn't sound interested.

"Well, I'm a junior at Sweet Valley High," Jessica said brightly, watching him for a reaction. Was he going to think she was too young? Because after getting a closer look at Chad, Jessica realized he was a few years *older* than she had estimated during their short conversation by the side of the road the other day.

"That's it?"

"Of course not," Jessica replied, with a playful toss of her hair. "I'm a cheerleader, I play tennis . . ." *Just don't raise the subject of photography!* she reminded herself. Chad hadn't mentioned the picture yet, and she hoped he'd forgotten about it. "I belong to a sorority at school, Pi Beta Alpha. I have a pretty typical family—parents, a sister, a brother—"

"And a dog," said Chad.

"Yeah." Elizabeth must have had Prince Albert with her that day at the beach, Jessica guessed. She had better divert Chad's attention from that particular recollection. "What about you?" she asked. "Do you go to school or work or what?"

Chad took a drag on his cigarette. Jessica saw his lips curve in another half-smile. Or was it a smirk? At first, she had thought that the look was sexy but now she was starting to find it annoying. "I work."

"Doing what?"

Chad glanced at her. "I'm an entrepreneur."

He didn't offer any further information, and Jessica got the feeling he wasn't planning to. *If he's not really interested in talking to me, then why did he ask me out?* she wondered, gripping the armrest as Chad speeded up to pass another car. Out of the corner of her eye, she studied his profile. Was he the strong, silent type, or was he a washout? *Well, even if he turns out to be a loser, he's still incredibly good-looking,* Jessica thought. As usual, she didn't have too much trouble seeing the bright side. Chad would be all right for one date. When she recapped the evening for her friends, she could always make it sound more exciting than it was.

"So, where are we going?" she asked him.

Chad tossed the cigarette butt out the window. "I thought I'd take you to some of my favorite places."

Jessica smiled happily. That sounded promising.

A moment later, Chad hit the blinker and pulled the light blue convertible off the road. Jessica stared in disbelief. *Valley Bowling?* This was one of Chad's favorite places? Was he kidding?

Apparently not. Chad got out of the car and waited for Jessica to let herself out and walk around to join him.

I did not spend an hour putting my hottest look together to go bowling! Jessica thought. She climbed out of the car, expressing her displeasure with an exasperated sigh.

Chad didn't seem to notice. "This'll be fun," he said through a cloud of cigarette smoke.

"Yeah, fun."

Valley Bowling looked tacky from the outside, and on the inside, it was even worse. It didn't exactly draw the most glamorous crowd either, Jessica observed. "Do you come here often?" she asked. This really couldn't be his idea of a special date. It wasn't too late for him to slap her on the shoulder, say it was a practical joke, and tell her he really planned to take her out for dinner and dancing.

"A few times since I got to the area," Chad answered. He walked over to a counter where shoes could be rented. "Here. What's your size?"

Jessica shook her head. There was no way she was going to put on a pair of those hideous two-toned bowling shoes. Who knew whose feet had been in them before? "Those really aren't my style," she said. "I'll stick with the shoes I'm wearing."

"They won't let you on the lanes in those."

Fine with me! Jessica was about to make an ironic remark to that effect, but something in Chad's expression stopped her. He stood watching her, smoking and not smiling. Where were the flirty looks he'd given her the other day when they met at the side of the road?

Jessica reluctantly told him her size. Then, after he handed the bowling shoes to her, she sat down on a bench and put them on. *OK, I'll bowl*, she thought. And then inspiration struck. *But that doesn't mean I'll bowl well!* Maybe she could get the message across to Chad that there were other things she did a whole lot better.

"This ball is so heavy," Jessica complained as she and Chad walked to the lane they had been assigned.

"It was the lightest one they had," he remarked, not sounding particularly sympathetic.

Chad bowled first and got a spare. Jessica wound up and rolled her ball. It bounced right into the gutter. "Oops!" she exclaimed. The ball returned to her. This time, she aimed so that it got halfway down the lane before ending up in the gutter again. "I'm getting closer!" she said cheerfully.

Chad recorded her zero on the score sheet. Then he bowled a strike.

Every couple of turns, Jessica knocked down a few pins for variety's sake. She went all out on her last turn of the game, flinging the ball right into the gutter and then clutching her shoulder. "Ouch!" She grimaced theatrically. "I think I dislocated something."

Chad put a hand on her shoulder and massaged it, none too gently. "I don't think so."

"Well, I'm not up to another game. Sorry."

"That's all right. I was just going to suggest getting something to eat. Ready for dinner?"

Jessica wasn't sure. What did he have in mind? A truck stop? A hot-dog stand? "I guess so," she answered unenthusiastically.

"I know a good place in Big Mesa," Chad told her as they returned their balls and shoes and walked out to the parking lot. He slung a heavy arm around her shoulders. "Right on the water. You'll like it."

Jessica looked up at Chad, and he smiled down at her. There was still something in his eyes she couldn't quite read, but maybe that was a plus. She had always been intrigued by guys with a little mystery about them. Maybe Chad would turn out all right after all.

Jessica brightened considerably as they drove toward Big Mesa. It was a pretty classy town. A restaurant there was bound to be better than Valley Bowling. It could hardly be worse!

"Does this look like the kind of place where one of the men in your photograph would hang out?" Todd asked Elizabeth as he parked the BMW in front of Rick's Place.

The restaurant was shingled and quaint. Elizabeth could see a deck to the side, strung with colored lights. Far below them, the Pacific Ocean glittered orange in the setting sun.

"I'm not sure."

Todd scanned the menu posted near the door and summed it up. "An upscale hamburger joint. Sounds good to me!"

"But before we eat, we have to do some sleuthing," Elizabeth reminded him.

The restaurant was only half full. Elizabeth glanced around the interior quickly. The decor was nautical, and it was dimly lit, but even so Elizabeth was able to determine that none of the three men from the photograph were at the bar or seated at any of the tables or booths.

The hostess greeted Todd and Elizabeth with a smile. "Table for two?"

Elizabeth nodded. "Can I ask you something first, though?" She pulled the photograph from her purse and showed it to the hostess. "I took this picture at the beach near here the other day and right afterward, I realized that one of the men had dropped his wristwatch. I'm trying to find him so I can return it. Do you recognize any of them?"

The hostess tapped the photograph with a long fingernail. "This young blond guy," she said. "He's been in here before."

Elizabeth's pulse quickened. "Recently?"

"A couple times in the past week or so," the hostess confirmed. "I've never seen the other two guys, though."

"The blond man," Elizabeth pressed. "Do you know anything about him? His name, or where he lives or works?"

"Can't help you there," the hostess replied. "You could ask Steve, the bartender, though. If anybody would know, Steve would."

But the bartender had no more information than the hostess. Seated at a booth near the rear of the restaurant, Elizabeth and Todd conversed in low voices across the tops of their open menus.

"Isn't it frustrating?" Elizabeth was excited and disappointed at the same time. "I feel as if we're really close to finding out more about those men and their possible connection to the drug inquiry in Washington. I just wish we could *do* something! It's so hard to wait."

"We have to, though," Todd said. "We don't have any more leads on this blond guy. The most we can hope for is that he'll show up tonight."

"I hope he does."

"Well, since we have some time to kill, let's go for broke," Todd proposed with a grin. "Start with an appetizer and work our way right through the whole menu!"

101

Through the next hour and a half, Elizabeth and Todd managed to polish off a plate of nachos, two salads, two burgers, an order of onion rings, and a pitcher of soda.

"I can't eat another bite," Elizabeth groaned as they examined the dessert menu.

"You have to order something if you want an excuse to sit at this table awhile longer."

"Maybe it's not worth it," she admitted. "If the blond man hasn't shown up by now, he's probably not going to. And what would we say to him if he did? Maybe I *am* just overreacting to all these events and coincidences."

"I say we give it another half an hour. After all, some people like to eat dinner on the late side," Todd reminded her. "How about we split a hot-fudge sundae? Come on, it's in the line of duty."

Elizabeth laughed. "Oh, all right."

When the waiter left with their dessert order, Todd took another look at the photograph. "You know, if these guys are drug dealers, wouldn't they avoid a place like this? Keep a low profile—"

"Todd!" Elizabeth whispered. Her eyes were like saucers and she was staring toward the front of the restaurant. "It's him!"

Todd turned in his chair. Sure enough, the

blond man from the picture had just entered Rick's Place and was speaking to the hostess.

He wasn't alone.

Elizabeth's jaw dropped. "Jessica!" she gasped.

Ten

"Maybe they're not together," Todd said. "They can't be!"

"They can and they are." Elizabeth gripped the edge of the table, her knuckles white. "The hostess is seating them at a booth on the other side of the restaurant!"

Todd glanced quickly across the restaurant, then faced Elizabeth again. "Do you think they saw us?"

Elizabeth shook her head. "They didn't even look this way. And in this dim light, I don't think they could see us unless they tried, which of course they won't because they don't know we're here. They don't have a mirror in their booth the way we do. See? There they are."

By looking in the mirror along one wall of

their booth, Elizabeth and Todd could see Jessica and Chad clearly, without having to crane their necks and stare blatantly across the restaurant.

"Explain this to me," Todd begged Elizabeth. "I'm completely baffled!"

Elizabeth felt somewhat overwhelmed herself, but the pieces of the puzzle were starting to fall into place. "The new boy Jessica was trying to tell me about the other day!"

"What new boy?"

"Someone named Chad. And Chad just happens to be the blond man from the beach!" Elizabeth exclaimed. "Oh, why didn't I listen to her when she tried to tell me about him?"

"Slow down and start at the beginning," Todd said calmly.

"It was last Thursday," Elizabeth explained. "Two days after I took the photograph. The same night I had dinner at your house and we saw the newscast about the Senate inquiry and Ron Hunter."

"And?" Todd prompted.

"And before I left for your house, Jessica was trying to tell me about some guy she'd met that afternoon. She said it was a great story and that I'd get a real kick out of it. But I didn't have time for her. I was so wrapped up in getting ready to go out. I guess I hurt her feelings because later when I asked about Chad, after he had called on Saturday while Jessica was out, she refused to talk about him." Elizabeth bit her lip. "If only I'd listened!"

The waiter delivered their sundae. Todd spooned into it, a wry smile on his face. "It's kind of funny, if you think about it. The whole time we were doing all that detective work trying to track this guy down, he was calling Jessica and setting up dates with her!"

Elizabeth frowned. "I don't think it's funny at all."

"We don't have any proof that he's anyone out of the ordinary," Todd reminded her. "They're just out for a hamburger."

"Don't you see?" Elizabeth sat forward, her elbows on the table. "This isn't a coincidence."

"It's not?"

"Chad must have run into Jessica someplace and have mistaken her for me! Jessica probably thought Chad just wanted to go out with her. She had no way of knowing that he was after something!"

"The photograph?"

"The photograph," Elizabeth confirmed.

The sundae was melting in the dish between them. Elizabeth and Todd were too absorbed in Jessica's predicament to eat it. "So, what do we do now?" Todd asked.

"I wish I knew." Elizabeth stared into the mirror, trying to read it as if it were a crystal ball. *Maybe everything's OK,* she thought hopefully. *They're just having a hamburger, like Todd said.* But Elizabeth knew Jessica too well. Elizabeth could tell by the way her twin was sitting with her shoulders pressed tensely against the back of the booth and a menu held out in front of her like a shield that she was uncomfortable. The certainty swept over Elizabeth like a wave. Jessica was in trouble.

"Todd, I'm worried."

"Look, Chad and Jessica are sitting in the middle of a restaurant," Todd pointed out. "He wouldn't have brought her here if he was planning to harm her in some way."

"We could go over there. Barge in on their date!" Elizabeth proposed.

"And run the risk of scaring off Chad and never finding out if he and those other two men are connected somehow to the drug ring?"

Elizabeth felt more confused than ever. She had no idea what course of action was best.

"Let's wait and watch a while longer," Todd suggested.

Elizabeth sank back in the booth, resigned to keeping her eyes glued to the image of Jessica and Chad in the mirror.

*   *   *

"What are you going to order?" Jessica asked. It was getting harder and harder to act as if she were having fun. Chad was bad company; he had hardly said two words since they entered the restaurant. And it wasn't that he was dumb or boring, Jessica had decided. There was something going on in his head; she just didn't know what it was.

"I can't make up my mind," Jessica chattered on. "The burgers all sound good, but so do the salads. You've eaten here before, right? What do you suggest?"

Chad's menu was still lying closed on the table in front of him. *He's not interested in food, and he's sure not interested in me*, Jessica thought. *What* is *he interested in?*

"So, Jessica." Chad's light blue eyes were trained steadily on her face. "You haven't said anything about it, but I know you're into photography. I've been looking forward to seeing the picture you took of my friends and me at the beach last week."

What was with this guy and Elizabeth's picture? Jessica wondered. *She* kept forgetting about it; why couldn't he?

"Oh, the picture!" Jessica gave Chad an apol-

108

ogetic, silly-me smile. "I don't have it with me. I guess it just slipped my mind."

Chad's face hardened in a dark scowl. "You told me you'd bring it."

Jessica blinked, stunned by the harsh tone of his voice. "I know, but I—I left it in the darkroom at school," she replied, hoping he would believe her and drop the subject.

Chad's expression grew more angry. "No, you didn't," he growled. "I've already looked there."

Jessica stared across the table at him. He'd already looked there? "What do you mean?" she asked, even though Chad's meaning was only too clear. *Chad is the person who broke into the Sweet Valley High darkroom!* But why? Why would anyone be so interested in a photograph?

But Jessica had no chance to speculate further. Chad reached across the table and gripped her wrist tightly. "I think we'd better find that picture, Jessica," he said quietly.

Jessica felt the blood drain from her face. Chad wasn't fooling around; his grip on her wrist was like a vise. Before her eyes, Chad had changed from a cute boy to a dangerous man.

Maybe it was time to tell the truth and get herself out of this very weird situation. Jessica swallowed with difficulty; her mouth was dry.

"Look, Chad. You've made a mistake. I didn't take that photograph. My twin sister did. *She* has it. I don't know anything about it!"

Even as she was saying it, Jessica realized it sounded like the phoniest excuse ever. Not surprisingly, Chad didn't buy it. "Let's go get that photo." Chad stood up, still holding onto her wrist. "And no more games, if you know what's good for you."

Jessica stood up, her knees barely supporting her. "No more games," Chad had said. *But this is a game of some sort*, Jessica thought, *and I don't know the rules.*

What was her next move going to be?

Todd drummed his fingers on the table while Elizabeth methodically tore her paper napkin to shreds. Their eyes didn't leave the mirror on the wall of their booth for even a moment.

Elizabeth was the first to detect the change in Jessica's and Chad's expressions. Chad's face had set in grim lines, and Jessica no longer looked uncomfortable. Now she looked scared.

As Elizabeth watched, Chad grabbed Jessica's arm. They stood up. They were going to leave the restaurant!

"Todd, there's something wrong!" Elizabeth

cried, panic in her voice. "We've got to help Jessica!"

Todd and Elizabeth stood up, and Todd fumbled in his wallet for money to pay the check. "Hurry!" Elizabeth urged.

Todd threw some bills on the table. "OK. Let's go!"

Elizabeth hadn't taken her eyes off Jessica and Chad, who by now had reached the exit. She hurried after them, dodging a startled waitress.

Chad and Jessica slipped out the door. An instant later, a huge mob of people crowded into Rick's Place.

"Kimball party of twenty-five," Elizabeth heard the hostess say. "They're setting up tables in the side room for you right now. It'll just be a few more minutes."

"Excuse me. Excuse me!" In her anxiety, Elizabeth was practically shouting.

A boy about her age playfully refused to step out of Elizabeth's path. "What's the hurry? Stick around and help me celebrate my birthday."

Todd put a hand on the boy's shoulder and shoved him aside. "Hey!" the boy exclaimed indignantly.

At last, Todd and Elizabeth tumbled through the door. "There they are!" Elizabeth cried. Jessica was just sliding into the passenger seat of a light blue convertible parked a few spaces behind the BMW. "Jessica!" she screamed. "Oh no, Todd. We're too late," Elizabeth said in despair. "She didn't hear me."

"We can follow them. She'll be all right," Todd assured her. "Come on!"

They dashed to the BMW and jumped in. Todd turned the key in the ignition. Elizabeth waited for the sound of the engine springing to life, but there was only silence.

A horrible feeling swept over Elizabeth. This couldn't be happening again, now of all times!

Todd tried again. Still, the engine wouldn't start. Todd cursed and hit the steering wheel with the palm of his hand.

"Keep trying!" Elizabeth urged desperately as she twisted in her seat to look out the rear window. Chad was making his getaway, and he was taking Jessica with him.

Chad's car pulled abreast of the BMW. At that moment, Jessica turned, glanced out the passenger side window, and looked right across Todd at Elizabeth.

Jessica's eyes widened with surprise. For a split second, the two sisters stared at each other. Then Elizabeth saw Jessica pointing discreetly at something. *Her cheerleading jacket*, Elizabeth thought. Why would she point to that?

Was Jessica trying to send her a signal of some kind?

Tires squealing, Chad sped out of the parking lot. Meanwhile, Todd was still trying unsuccessfully to start the BMW. Elizabeth closed her eyes and directed her whole heart and soul into a single wish. *Start. Please start!*

A few seconds later, the BMW's engine roared to life. Elizabeth nearly fainted with joy. "They got a head start, but we'll catch them," Todd said with confidence. "Nothing can outrun this car."

"Chad turned left," Elizabeth told her boyfriend as he prepared to pull onto the main road. "Hurry, Todd!"

Todd pressed his foot against the gas pedal. In front of them, the highway appeared empty. For a moment, Elizabeth had a sinking feeling that she had made a mistake. Had Chad actually headed in the opposite direction?

Then a car came into view ahead of them. A blue convertible. It was Chad's! "Here we go!" Todd urged even more speed out of the BMW.

Todd zoomed up right behind the convertible and flashed his lights. But instead of slowing down, Chad hit the gas. "He's not going to stop!" Elizabeth exclaimed. "He knows we're chasing him!"

"I don't think he knows who we are. He just

thinks I'm some guy who wants to drag race him." Todd laughed grimly. "Well, if he wants a race, I'll give him one!"

Elizabeth held her breath as Todd put his foot all the way down on the gas pedal. Both cars hurtled down the highway at frightening speed, the BMW gaining ground. There was no one approaching from the opposite direction, so Todd crossed into the left lane, prepared to pull alongside Chad's car and force him over to the side of the road.

At that moment, Todd glanced into the rear-view mirror and saw the flashing lights of a police car. "Don't look now, but we're in trouble."

"Oh, no," she groaned.

"Sorry, Liz, but I have to pull over."

Todd braked and brought the BMW to a stop in a cloud of dust.

The state police cruiser pulled onto the shoulder behind the BMW. Todd rolled down his window as the police officer approached. "Before I write out a speeding ticket, maybe you can tell me what the rush is all about," the officer said sternly.

Elizabeth leaned across Todd. "My sister's being kidnapped!" Her voice caught on a sob.

Todd confirmed Elizabeth's story. "She's in

the car I was chasing. That's why I was driving so fast."

"She's in terrible trouble," Elizabeth continued. "The man she's with may be involved with drugs!"

Elizabeth had never been so serious in her life. The police officer must have sensed this. "Do you have any idea where they're going?" he asked.

Todd shook his head. Elizabeth was about to admit her ignorance, too, when suddenly she remembered Jessica, in Chad's car, pointing to her jacket.

"Wait a minute!" Jessica *had* been trying to send her twin a message, and Elizabeth knew what it was. Jessica had pointed to the letters on her cheerleading jacket: SVH. "They're going to Sweet Valley High!"

Eleven

Jessica hadn't been able to believe her eyes when she glimpsed Todd's car in the parking lot. What on earth had brought Elizabeth and Todd to Rick's Place? Could it have been the same thing that had brought Jessica there—Chad?

Elizabeth knew something was wrong. Jessica had seen that much during the brief moment their eyes had met. So Jessica had done the first thing that popped into her mind. She had pointed to the letters on her cheerleading jacket, hoping Elizabeth and Todd would figure out the clue and follow her and Chad to Sweet Valley High.

Chad had warned her against playing any more games with him, but Jessica hadn't had

116

any choice. As they had left the restaurant, she had fibbed once more, this time telling Chad the photograph was in her locker at school. Of course, it wasn't, but Jessica supposed there was a slight chance that the picture was in *Elizabeth's* locker, and Jessica knew her sister's combination.

And I'm playing with fire, Jessica thought now, glancing at Chad out of the corner of her eye. His eyes were narrowed against the smoke from his cigarette, and his jaw was set hard as rock. What would he do when he found out she had misled him again?

Todd and Liz will rescue me. Jessica flipped down the passenger-side visor, pretending to check her hair in the small mirror clipped there. Angling the mirror, she got a view of the highway behind them. Her heart lifted. Todd's BMW was catching up!

Suddenly Jessica felt the convertible surge forward. Jessica watched the speedometer climb. Did Chad suspect something? "Why are you driving so fast?" she asked him. It was the first time she had dared open her mouth since they got in the car, and her voice came out in a nervous, high-pitched tone.

"Some rich kid showing off his fancy foreign car," Chad said scornfully. "Thinks he can make me eat his dust. *Nobody* passes me."

Jessica relaxed somewhat. Chad was just being macho. As if his dumpy old car were any match for a brand-new BMW! There was no way Chad would be able to shake off Elizabeth and Todd.

Jessica risked a look at the BMW, just in time to see the flashing lights of the police car. Chad laughed triumphantly. "Poor little rich boy's going to get a speeding ticket. What a shame."

Jessica twisted in her seat and watched in despair as Todd's car receded into the distance. A speeding ticket would tie up Elizabeth and Todd for ages! They would never catch up with Chad now.

I'm on my own with him, Jessica realized, the last of her optimism fading. *No one can help me now. I'm going to have to help myself.*

Chad was wearing that half-smile again. Jessica guessed he was pleased with himself for having ditched Todd with a speeding ticket.

Chad's half-smile gave her the creeps. She couldn't believe she ever found it, or him, attractive. Jessica felt that it was time to satisfy her curiosity. She might as well ask; at this point, she had nothing to lose.

She took a deep breath. "So, why do you want to see this picture so badly? It's nothing special. It's just a—picture."

Chad looked at her as he lit another cigarette. "You're nosy, you know that? You take too many pictures, and you ask too many questions."

Just one picture and one question! Jessica thought with indignation. Prudently, she kept her mouth shut.

Chad laughed cruelly. "Yeah, you should really watch out, Jessica. You could get yourself in trouble someday."

Someday might arrive sooner than you think, she thought unhappily. *Like when I open Elizabeth's locker and there's no photo!*

Jessica had one last hope, that there would be something going on at Sweet Valley High that night. A band or chorus rehearsal, anything. If there were other people around, maybe she would be able to give Chad the slip. And if she couldn't get away, at least he wouldn't harm her in front of witnesses.

Chad chose a spot on the edge of the Sweet Valley High parking lot. He held Jessica's arm as they walked toward the school, his fingers digging into the flesh above her elbow. "Just show me where to go," he instructed her.

Jessica could see that, except for security night lighting, the school building was dark. She stopped in her tracks. "I just thought of something. We're not going to be able to get in. The school's all locked up!"

Apparently, Chad found her remark very humorous. Jessica heard the cruel laugh again. It made her skin crawl. "We'll get to your locker." Chad tugged on her arm to force her to keep walking. "Don't you worry."

When they reached the main entrance of the school, Chad stopped in front of one of the windows. Before Jessica knew what was happening, he had kicked it in.

"What are you doing?" Jessica screamed, hoping someone would hear her.

"Shut up," Chad barked. "Get inside." When Jessica hesitated, he gave her a rough push. "Now!"

Jessica climbed through the broken window into the dark lobby. She was shaking. Now that she had seen Chad's violence in action, she was more frightened than ever.

"Lead the way," Chad ordered, giving Jessica another push.

Sweet Valley High was a maze of corridors, and Jessica purposefully took the long way around to Elizabeth's locker. Maybe she would find somebody else in the school building; maybe someone would discover the break-in and investigate.

And maybe the photograph will *be in Liz's locker*, Jessica thought, hoping against hope. Once he had what he wanted, he would leave her alone, wouldn't he?

"This is it," Jessica said, stopping in front of Elizabeth's locker.

"Get to it, then. You've wasted enough of my time already."

Jessica put her hand on the dial of the combination lock. She stooped and squinted to read the numbers in the dim night lighting. She turned the dial to the right, then to the left. But her hand was shaking so badly she overshot the second number in Elizabeth's combination.

"What's taking so long?" Chad snapped.

"I—I messed up."

"Get it right!" Chad yelled. He kicked the locker, and the metallic crash echoed down the deserted hallway.

Jessica jumped at the noise and quickly spun the dial. But it was harder than ever to read the numbers on the lock because her eyes had filled with tears.

She misdialed again. "I'm sorry," she said, brushing the tears from her cheeks. "This time I'll—"

"Clear out of the way!" Chad shoved Jessica aside. He kicked again at the locker, striking the lock hard with his boot heel. Jessica stood frozen with terror. It was apparent that Chad

121

was desperate enough to rip the door of the locker right off with his bare hands.

Suddenly a bright light illuminated the corridor. "Hold it right there!" a deep voice commanded.

Jessica whirled to face the light, one hand raised to shield her eyes. Men in blue uniforms—the police!

Chad turned in the opposite direction and sprinted at top speed away from the police spotlight. Away from the police, but straight into Todd!

Todd jumped out from behind a bank of lockers and tackled Chad to the ground. Chad and Todd rolled over and over, locked in a fierce struggle. Jessica screamed. Chad was choking Todd!

With a grunt, Todd thrust Chad off. An instant later, Todd had pinned Chad, just in time for the policeman who had rushed to the grappling pair to snap handcuffs on Chad's wrists.

Jessica slumped against the lockers, not sure whether to laugh or cry. Then she saw Elizabeth hurrying toward her with another policeman. "Jess, are you all right?" Elizabeth cried, throwing her arms around her sister.

"Oh, Liz!" Jessica hugged her sister with all her might.

"Don't worry," Elizabeth said soothingly. "You're safe. We came after you."

"I knew you would!" Jessica smiled at her twin through her tears. "But did you have to cut it so close?"

Todd and Elizabeth had followed the police to the high school. Now Jessica joined her sister and Todd in the BMW, and once more they tailed the police car, this time to the Sweet Valley police station.

"Is someone going to tell me what's going on?" Jessica demanded, leaning forward from the backseat to stick her face in between Elizabeth's and Todd's.

Elizabeth was glad to see that her sister appeared to be recovering rapidly from her scare. "Todd and I don't know much more than you do," she admitted.

"But Chad." Jessica shivered as she spoke the name. "Who is he? What is this photograph he's so concerned about? And why did you take it?"

"It's a long story, and I think it's going to get longer," Elizabeth predicted. "Chad's the one with the answers. The police are going to question him, and we'll hear what he has to say for himself."

"I'll tell you one thing," Jessica said, shaking her head. "That's the last time I go out with a total stranger just because he's cute, and it's also the last time I let somebody think I'm you. Talk about a double whammy!"

Todd parked in front of the station, and the three hurried inside. An officer ushered them into a conference room, where a glowering Chad was already seated between two policemen. Jessica clutched Elizabeth's hand, and Elizabeth gave Jessica's a supportive squeeze.

"Twins," Chad muttered. "I should've known. Twins have caused me nothing but trouble."

Detective Meyers, chief of the Sweet Valley police force, conducted the questioning. "You've been informed of your rights," he began, "and I'd like to inform you of something else. An FBI team is on its way. You might as well give us the story now. It will be a good rehearsal. Ms. Wakefield, can I have the photograph?"

Elizabeth handed Detective Meyers the photograph and told him the date she had taken it. Detective Meyers in turn showed it to Chad. "This is the reason you abducted Miss Wakefield and broke into Sweet Valley High, isn't it?"

At the sight of the photograph, Chad's rage bubbled to the surface once again. "That idiot

Ron Hunter!" he burst out. "If it hadn't been for him—"

"Ron Hunter!" Elizabeth exclaimed.

"Who's Ron Hunter?" Jessica wanted to know.

"Ron Hunter is the key witness in a drug inquiry currently underway in the Senate," Detective Meyers informed her. "Can you explain to us how Ron Hunter could have been on the beach in Sweet Valley with you, at the very same time he was testifying in Washington, D.C.?"

"Twins," Chad answered with a bitter laugh. "That's Ron Hunter in the picture, all right. The guy in Washington pretending to be Ron is his twin brother, Rich."

"Identical twins!" Elizabeth whispered to Todd. "Of course! Why didn't I, of all people, think of that?"

Chad paused in his story and looked down at the handcuffs on his wrists. *He has to recognize how serious his situation is,* Elizabeth imagined. *He's trapped—he might as well talk.*

Chad took a deep breath and continued. "Ron and Rich were both involved with us, selling drugs."

"Drugs?" Jessica asked Elizabeth in a whisper.

"Just listen!" Elizabeth whispered back.

"But Ron went soft on us. Said he didn't want to make money from ruining people's lives anymore. So he got out of it and turned informer. He blew the whistle on us. The biggest operation in the country, and the government had no idea we even existed until he told them," Chad said with perverse pride. "We came up with a way to stop him before he could name names, though. We kidnapped him before he could give the rest of us away."

"And his brother Rich took Ron's place in order to change the testimony and protect you," Detective Meyers surmised.

"You got it. It would have worked, too." Chad turned his hostile gaze on Jessica and Elizabeth. "If it hadn't been for her—or her? Whichever one it was on the beach that day!"

Elizabeth closed her eyes. For a few seconds, she felt transported back to that afternoon at the beach when she'd been taking pictures with Regina's camera. The three men running with Ron Hunter in the middle . . .

"He escaped!" Elizabeth exclaimed.

"That's right," Chad said. "We made the mistake of treating the guy like an old friend instead of the back-stabbing traitor he really is. Took him for a drive to get some fresh air. We were at a stoplight near the beach, and the next thing we knew he jumped right out of the car and made a break for it. Me and George chased him halfway down the beach before we caught him." Chad pointed in the twins' direction. "That's when you—or you—blew it all by popping out of nowhere to take our picture!"

"You had a good reason for wanting to get your hands on the photograph," Detective Meyers observed.

"You're telling me," Chad snorted. "With Ron's, I mean Rich's face on every TV channel, we couldn't risk that picture being seen."

"You know, I might never have noticed the resemblance between the man in my photograph and the man on TV," Elizabeth spoke up, "if your friend hadn't made such a big deal about my having taken the picture in the first place. That's what made me suspicious."

"At first we thought the only thing we could do was cross our fingers that nothing would come of it. And then I spotted your sister." Chad smiled coldly at Jessica. Elizabeth felt Jessica tense. "It seemed like a great chance to get hold of the picture and destroy the evidence. I suppose you two think you're pretty smart, leading me right into a trap!"

Elizabeth and Jessica exchanged an amused glance. If Chad only knew!

"I think we've heard enough for now," Detective Meyers announced. "You can lock him up," he instructed the other officers.

Chad left the room in custody. Elizabeth, Jessica, and Todd got to their feet. "We'll need to talk to you again tomorrow," Detective Meyers told the twins. "For now, I'd just like to shake your hands. You've done the whole country a great service."

"It was just luck," Elizabeth said as she shook Detective Meyers's hand. "I guess I was in the right place at the right time!"

"You and your camera." Jessica laughed. "And I just thought you were being a real pain lately, taking pictures of everything under the sun. I didn't realize you were catching criminals!"

My camera and me, Elizabeth thought. Then she corrected herself. *Regina's camera and me*. It looked as if together they had accomplished some pretty important work.

Twelve

"That's twice you've been on national TV in a matter of weeks," observed Amy at lunch two days later.

"I know," said Jessica complacently. "Isn't it something?"

Of course, Eric Parker's talk show about a month back didn't really count. Due to an underhanded trick of Lila's, Jessica was prevented from appearing on the show, and Eric had actually interviewed Elizabeth, pretending to be Jessica. *Sort of like Ron and Rich Hunter!* Jessica reflected. But of course Amy didn't know that. Only Jessica, Elizabeth, and Todd knew the truth behind that episode. But last night's TV appearance had been for real. The day after Chad's arrest and the subsequent release of the real Ron Hunter, Rich Hunter had broken down and confessed as well. The huge drug operation had been busted wide open, and Jessica, Elizabeth, and Todd were mentioned in all the news reports.

"How does it feel to be a hero?" class clown Winston Egbert asked, sticking an imaginary microphone under Jessica's nose.

"I don't think of myself as a hero," Jessica answered, with an air of noble humility. "I think of myself as an ordinary citizen, doing my small part to keep this beautiful nation free of crime and vice."

"Spare us," Lila groaned. "Liz is the one who was trying to track down criminals. You were just trying to get a date!"

"Be that as it may," Jessica replied, "I helped!"

"A lot of great things are done by accident," Winston pointed out to Lila. "That doesn't make them any less important."

Lila yawned, a look of indescribable boredom on her face. Lila always pouted when Jessica was in the spotlight. Jessica was sure that in a moment or two, Lila would remind them all of her bit role in Jamie Peters's upcoming movie. Jessica thought she had better answer Winston and cut Lila off before she got started. "So true." She smiled broadly at Lila and then took a big bite of her sandwich.

"Make way," Winston announced. "More heroes to starboard."

The group at the lunch table shifted to make room for Todd, Elizabeth, and Shelley. "I don't think I qualify," Shelley said.

"Sure you do," Winston told her. "You still possess hero status from helping the girls' basketball team win the county championship."

"That was awhile ago, though," Shelley reminded him.

"No problem," Winston insisted. "Hero status lasts for six months. After that, it has to be renewed with another heroic act."

Shelley laughed. "Oh, is that how it works?"

"Take it from Winston," said his girlfriend, Maria Santelli, "Sweet Valley High's champion opportunist."

Elizabeth put down her lunch tray. On it were a sandwich, an apple, a bottle of seltzer, and her camera.

"There it is," Winston said, holding his hand over his heart. "The camera that caught a thousand criminals."

"The camera that drove a thousand people crazy," Jessica corrected him. "Please tell us you're going to let us eat our lunch in peace," she begged her sister, "and not take pictures of us chewing and swallowing!"

"Chew and swallow all you want," Elizabeth replied. "I promise I'm not working on a photographic series entitled 'My Sister Eating Her Lunch.' "

"And what *are* you working on?" Todd asked.

Elizabeth raised her eyebrows at him, and Todd laughed. "I thought maybe crime fighting had distracted you and you might have let your guard down," he teased.

"No such luck!"

But the Ron Hunter adventure *had* been a distraction. While she and Todd had been busy pursuing the mystery of the three men on the beach, Elizabeth had almost forgotten about the photography club's project. Now, she was making up for lost time. The club would be putting the photo essay together in only a few days.

"I missed the last photography club meeting," Elizabeth said to Shelley. During that meeting on Monday, she and Todd had been at Mr. Sutton's studio. "Although I suppose nothing much happened because the darkroom was still shut down."

Shelley just shrugged.

"But I bumped into Jim earlier today," Elizabeth continued, "and he said that although some of the equipment was damaged beyond repair and will have to be replaced, the rest of it is back in service for our meeting today." She smiled. "He was pretty excited!"

"I'm sure."

Elizabeth was surprised by Shelley's sarcastic tone. Was something wrong between her and Jim? *I'll have to find out about this another time*, Elizabeth decided. The crowded cafeteria wasn't the place for a private conversation.

"Seriously, though, Jessica," Maria was saying. "That horrible Chad person was a real desperado. He could have killed you! Weren't you scared?"

"Not at all," Jessica answered, ignoring Elizabeth's dubious look. "Chad wasn't going to kill me as long as he thought I had what he wanted." That much was true. "I was just waiting for my opportunity to gain the upper hand. If Liz and the police hadn't shown up when they did, I was going to improvise a few karate moves. You know, Maria, variations on some of our cheerleading kicks."

"Right. I would have liked to see that!" Lila burst out. "Then I suppose you were going to tie him up with your shoelaces, sling him over your shoulder, and deliver him to the police station yourself!"

"Exactly," replied Jessica with a grin.

Just then, Elizabeth spotted Ms. Bellasario, a music teacher, sitting with a group of students. Ms. Bellasario had arranged several half-full seltzer bottles in a row. Using a spoon, she was improvising a tune on the bottles and making the students laugh.

That would make a great picture for the photo essay! thought Elizabeth. She grabbed her camera and stood up. As she did, she glanced at Shelley who was looking at Jim, sitting with some of his photography club friends a few tables away.

The expression on Shelley's face spoke volumes. She looked resentful and hurt and wistful all at the same time. Elizabeth made a mental note. The next mystery she'd solve would be the one concerning Jim and Shelley!

"This is it, you guys," Jim announced to the members of the photography club who were assembled at the school on Saturday morning. "Everybody stake out a space and go to it!"

Mr. Marks had cleared everything with Mr. Cooper. The photography club was free to use the entire north wall of the lobby for their mural. First, they had tacked an enormous piece of plastic sheeting to the four corners of the wall. Now, equipped with stepladders, glue guns, and their photographs, the club was ready to start.

It's going to be wonderful, Jim thought, walking behind the row of busily working students. Everyone's pictures were so different! Claire's were hilarious. She had snuck into the boys' locker room and caught the football team in their towels. Andy's photographs were sensitive studies of interracial friendships at Sweet Valley High, and included a beautiful portrait of Patty and DeeDee. Meanwhile, DeeDee had recorded the life of the arts at Sweet Valley High: students painting, sculpting, and acting. Neil's pictures were of students standing in the cafeteria lunch line and making gruesome faces. Allen's were group shots: the cheerleaders in a pyramid, the chorus posed on risers rehearsing for a concert, a crowd at a sports event.

Jim stopped next to Elizabeth. "There's space here for your pictures," she told him. "Hey, you know, that reminds me. You never did say what your special angle for the mural was going to be."

Jim handed her a stack of photographs. "See for yourself."

Elizabeth flipped through them and smiled. "They're of *us*!" Jim had caught the photography club in action in the darkroom, printing pictures and talking to one another about their

135

work. A picture of herself made Elizabeth laugh. "I don't remember you taking this."

"None of you guys noticed me clicking away at you. I guess when you're used to pointing a camera yourself, you don't notice when someone points one at you."

"Well, they're great," Elizabeth pronounced, returning the pictures to him.

"Yours turned out pretty well, too."

"I think so," Elizabeth admitted. "I just hope it's not too obvious which teachers I like best!"

"Not *too* obvious," Jim said, indicating a nine-by-twelve of Mr. Collins.

For a few minutes, the two worked side by side in silence. Jim felt comfortable with Elizabeth, and a few times he cleared his throat, as if he were on the verge of confiding in her. He hadn't talked to anybody yet about his falling-out with Shelley. He was almost afraid to admit that it might be more than just a quarrel. But he was starting to worry. Every day in school, Shelley gave him the brush-off, and lately when he called her at home, she always had something to do or somewhere to go that prevented her from talking to him. Was she spending her time with Greg Hilliard now?

Before Jim got around to breaking the silence, Elizabeth spoke up. "I've really learned a lot from the photography club so far. Working on the photo essay and taking pictures on my own has sharpened my powers of observation, you know? Photography will probably make me a better writer in the long run."

"Right. It's like the name of your newspaper column, 'Eyes and Ears.' You have to look *and* listen for good stories."

"I just never thought one little photograph could be so powerful," Elizabeth mused.

"I know what you mean. The picture you took of Ron Hunter and the two other men helped solve a major crime! It really makes you think."

"I guess there's something behind that expression, a picture is worth a thousand words. Although as a writer," Elizabeth added, "I don't know if I can completely endorse that!"

She stepped back to get a perspective on the photographs she had arranged so far. "The mural's been fun, but I suppose you'll be glad when it's finished. It's taken up a lot of your time, hasn't it?"

"You're not kidding," Jim grunted. The next thing he knew, he had blurted out the whole story of how the secret photography club project had gotten him in trouble with Shelley. "Now she's shutting *me* out. I can't get through to her."

Elizabeth was sympathetic. "I thought maybe

something like that had happened. I had to fend off Todd, too. And my sister!"

"I'm hoping she'll understand when she sees the photo essay," Jim said, aiming the glue gun, "that I had a reason for excluding her from part of my life for a while. I don't want to lose her." His voice was quiet but intense.

"Well, why don't you make sure she understands?" suggested Elizabeth. "A picture's worth a thousand words, remember? Shelley will be looking at the mural along with everybody else. Put up a picture that will get a special message across to her."

"Liz, you're a genius," Jim declared, giving her a spontaneous hug. "And I think I know exactly which picture to use!"

Thirteen

Something was going on at Sweet Valley High. Shelley could see that as soon as she entered the main lobby with Greg and Cathy on Monday morning. A crowd of students was gathered at the north wall, buzzing and laughing.

"What *is* that?" Shelley asked, staring ahead at the wall that was papered with photographs, large and small, color and black-and-white.

"It looks like some kind of mural," Cathy observed.

"Let's check it out!" said Greg.

They joined the rest of the students who were examining the mural. In the center was a sign. "The Many Faces of Sweet Valley High: A Photo Essay," Shelley read out loud. So *this* was the photography club's project!

I should boycott it on principle, Shelley thought, remembering how annoyed and hurt she had been by Jim's secretiveness. But she couldn't make herself turn away. The mural had already captured her attention.

Everyone was laughing and pointing, locating pictures of themselves and their friends. Greg grabbed Shelley's arm. "Now there's a handsome guy, huh?"

Shelley doubled over with laughter at the picture of Greg in the lunch line with his tongue out and eyes crossed. "I wondered why Neil was asking us what we thought of the cafeteria food," said Greg. "I thought maybe he was compiling evidence to petition for better chow!"

"Here's one of me!" Cathy cried, delighted. "In chemistry lab."

"I can hardly recognize you with those goggles on." Shelley laughed. "You look like a mad scientist!"

"Did you notice how this was put together?" Cathy asked Shelley as they wandered along the wall. "It looks as if each person in the photography club constructed one section. See?" They stopped, and Cathy pointed to DeeDee Gordon's name. "And everybody has a theme. All of DeeDee's pictures are kind of artsy."

"So everyone who worked on the mural contributed something personal to it," Shelley remarked.

"And I bet everyone who *looks* at it gets something personal out of it, too," Cathy mused. "It tells a different story, depending on who's reading it."

Cathy was already a little ahead of Shelley. "Oh, Shell, you've got to see these." Cathy hauled her over to Claire Middleton's photos. "The football team looks even better in their towels than in their uniforms, don't you think?"

Shelley smiled thoughtfully. All of a sudden, Jim's behavior made sense. The photo essay wouldn't have been nearly as effective if people had known about it beforehand. Now everyone was completely open to the mural. It surprised them into looking at Sweet Valley High in new ways.

But that realization didn't automatically repair the rift between Shelley and Jim. *We haven't really talked in days*, she thought. The photography club had taken over Jim's life. He had a lot of new friends, and for all Shelley knew, he was just as happy without her. She knew she had contributed to the tense situation, too, by overreacting at the Dairi Burger the other day and by avoiding him. *It's because I'm afraid of what he might say*, she realized. *I don't know what he thinks. I don't know what he wants.*

Suddenly Shelley found herself staring at Jim's name. These were the pictures he'd taken! *Of the kids in the photography club—of course*, she thought bitterly. Then she realized that one of the pictures, the one right in the middle of Jim's section, was different.

It was the picture he had entered in the *Sweet Valley News* photography contest, the first-prize picture of Shelley playing basketball, the photograph that had played a pivotal role in their falling in love.

For a long moment, Shelley just stood gazing at it. *The photo essay tells a different story, depending on who's reading it. . . .*

Shelley knew what that photograph meant, to her and Jim both. It told her that Jim loved her as much as ever, that she still held first place in his heart.

She turned on her heel and bumped right into Jim. "So, what do you think?" he asked, shuffling his feet as if he were nervous about her verdict.

For an answer, Shelley put her arms around Jim's neck and lifted her mouth to his for a kiss.

"Now do you forgive me for keeping secrets from you?" Elizabeth asked Jessica as they stood side by side in front of the photography club's mural.

"Well, I forgive Allen Walters for spying on the cheerleaders." Jessica paused to admire how well Allen's photo of the squad had come out, particularly, how attractive she herself looked. "But not you," she teased her sister. "*Your* picture-taking almost got me killed!"

"You put yourself in danger," Elizabeth countered. "If you'd only told me you were considering dating one of the three men from the beach, I would have warned you!"

They were joking about it now, but Elizabeth knew that if Jessica had suffered any harm at Chad's hands, she would never have forgiven herself.

"It wouldn't have worked anyway," Jessica said and shrugged. "If you'd warned me about Chad, I would have been even more determined to go out with him!"

Elizabeth laughed. Suddenly Todd came up behind her and wrapped his strong arms around her. "It's beautiful," Todd breathed into Elizabeth's hair. "I'm incredibly impressed."

"Really?" Elizabeth twisted around to see Todd's expression.

His dark brown eyes were glowing with love and pride. "Really. Your pictures are practically the best up there."

"What do you mean *practically* the best?" Elizabeth demanded.

"Tina Ayala took the prize-winning photo in my opinion, that's all," Todd replied, pulling Elizabeth toward Tina's section.

Elizabeth smiled. Tina had focused on Sweet Valley High sweethearts, and Elizabeth thought she knew which picture Todd was referring to.

Tina had taken the picture at a soccer game. Todd and Elizabeth were watching from the sidelines, and Todd had lifted Elizabeth onto his broad shoulders so she would have a better view. It had been a hilarious moment, and the photograph had captured their happiness.

"A pretty happy couple, wouldn't you say?" Todd whispered into Elizabeth's ear.

She nodded. "A very happy couple."

Holding hands, they wandered to the other end of the mural. At that moment, Elizabeth's attention was caught by two people just entering the school building. "Todd, look!" she exclaimed. "It's Mr. and Mrs. Morrow! What do you think they're doing here? Come on, let's go say hello."

Todd and Elizabeth made their way across the crowded lobby. "Mr. and Mrs. Morrow, hi," Elizabeth called.

Mrs. Morrow greeted Elizabeth with a warm

smile. "Hello, Liz. I see you've been putting Regina's camera to good use!"

"I'll say!" Elizabeth confirmed. "I can't thank you enough. It was a wonderful gift."

"Congratulations," Mr. Morrow said to Elizabeth and Todd. "The whole town is talking about your detective work, and your bravery."

"It was all Liz."

"I stumbled into it," Elizabeth said modestly. "I'm just glad it ended well. But what brings you to Sweet Valley High? Did Andrea tell you about the mural?"

"Actually she did, and we'd like to see her photos," Mrs. Morrow replied. "But we're also here to talk with Mr. Cooper about making a gift to the school."

"We heard about the destruction that was done to the darkroom," Mr. Morrow explained. "We'd like to donate funds to re-equip the facility."

"That's so generous!" Elizabeth exclaimed.

"It would make us happy to do something for the photography club," Mrs. Morrow continued. "If Regina were alive, she would have been an enthusiastic member."

Elizabeth was moved. "What a beautiful gesture."

Talking about her daughter had brought an expression of sadness to Mrs. Morrow's face but now she brightened. "Show us your pictures, Liz!"

Elizabeth led them to her section of the mural. One picture caused Mrs. Morrow to wipe a tear from her eye. It was the photograph of Elizabeth and Regina that Mrs. Morrow had given to Elizabeth along with the camera.

Mrs. Morrow gently tapped the photograph. "Why did you include this one?"

"Because as I've used her camera, I've felt as if Regina were at my side," Elizabeth said. "We did this together. Regina contributed to this photo essay as much as any of us."

Mrs. Morrow gave Elizabeth a quick hug. "That makes me feel good. Come on, Kurt. Let's go see"—Mrs. Morrow smiled through her tears—"what did Nicholas and Regina always call him? Chrome Dome Cooper!"

After Elizabeth said goodbye to the Morrows, she couldn't get the conversation that had just taken place out of her mind. Suddenly she had a rush of insight. "Todd, do you think it might have been partly due to my memory of Regina, and the fact that I was using her camera, that I felt so driven to discover the connection between the photo of the three men on the beach and the news story about the drug ring?"

"You mean because drugs caused Regina's death?"

Elizabeth nodded. "It's almost as if, in a weird sort of way, some justice has been done. With the help of Regina's camera, a major drug ring was exposed! Who knows how many lives have been saved?"

She and Todd gazed thoughtfully at the picture for a moment longer. Before they turned away, Elizabeth whispered softly, "Thanks, Regina."

"Donut, anybody?" Amy Sutton offered the box to her friends.

Jessica had stopped to gab with some of the other cheerleaders in front of Allen Walters's section of the photo essay.

"I don't know how it happens," Amy said, shaking her head. "There I am, innocently driving to school, and the next thing I know, my car has parked itself in front of Caster's Bakery."

"I know that syndrome," Cara said, giggling. "You don't even remember going in and buying anything, but there's the evidence: a dozen donuts riding in your passenger seat."

"Let's eat them, not talk about them!" Jessica declared, helping herself to a chocolate donut.

Maria and Cara dug in as well. Robin Wilson

put out her hand and then pulled it back. Then with a sigh, she grabbed a jelly donut.

"One donut's not going to hurt you," Jessica told her. *Not that I'd risk it if I were Robin*, she thought. If she had been fat once the way Robin had, Jessica was sure she would limit herself to carrot sticks for the rest of her life.

Not that anyone would know from looking at Robin now, what she used to look like. Now Robin was one of the most beautiful girls at Sweet Valley High and co-captain of the cheerleaders.

Robin bit into her donut, one eye on the picture Allen had taken of the cheerleading squad performing their pyramid. "Maybe I shouldn't eat this," she joked. "Or I'll have to move to the bottom row of the pyramid."

"Hey, I'm in the bottom row!" Amy said, pretending to be insulted.

Jessica guessed this might be one of those times when Robin wanted somebody to reassure her that she didn't have to worry about her weight anymore. *Well, I'm not going to bother.* Jessica selected another donut. Robin didn't really have anything to worry about. She was a knockout, a Sweet Valley High cheerleader and champion diver. Plus, Robin had a gorgeous boyfriend, college freshman George Warren, who was absolutely devoted to her. As far as Jessica could see, Robin's life was picture perfect. *Maybe I'm the one who shouldn't be gobbling these donuts!* Jessica thought.

"Come on. It's time for homeroom," Amy announced, strolling away with the bakery box. The other girls followed, Robin casting one last glance over her shoulder at the photograph on the wall.

Will Robin's past come back to haunt her? Find out in Sweet Valley High #74, **THE PERFECT GIRL.**

☐ 27650	**AGAINST THE ODDS #51**	$2.95
☐ 27720	**WHITE LIES #52**	$2.95
☐ 27771	**SECOND CHANCE #53**	$2.95
☐ 27856	**TWO BOY WEEKEND #54**	$2.95
☐ 27915	**PERFECT SHOT #55**	$2.95
☐ 27970	**LOST AT SEA #56**	$2.95
☐ 28079	**TEACHER CRUSH #57**	$2.95
☐ 28156	**BROKEN HEARTS #58**	$2.95
☐ 28193	**IN LOVE AGAIN #59**	$2.95
☐ 28264	**THAT FATAL NIGHT #60**	$2.95
☐ 28317	**BOY TROUBLE #61**	$2.95
☐ 28352	**WHO'S WHO #62**	$2.95
☐ 28385	**THE NEW ELIZABETH #63**	$2.95
☐ 28487	**THE GHOST OF TRICIA MARTIN #64**	$2.95
☐ 28518	**TROUBLE AT HOME #65**	$2.95
☐ 28555	**WHO'S TO BLAME #66**	$2.95
☐ 28611	**THE PARENT PLOT #67**	$2.95
☐ 28618	**THE LOVE BET #68**	$2.95
☐ 28636	**FRIEND AGAINST FRIEND #69**	$2.95
☐ 28767	**MS. QUARTERBACK #70**	$2.95
☐ 28796	**STARRING JESSICA #71**	$2.95
☐ 28841	**ROCK STAR'S GIRL #72**	$2.95
☐ 28863	**REGINA'S LEGACY #73**	$2.95

Series
Don't miss any of the Caitlin trilogies
Created by Francine Pascal

There has never been a heroine quite like the raven-haired, unforgettable beauty, Caitlin. Dazzling, charming, rich, and very, very clever Caitlin Ryan seems to have everything. Everything, that is, but the promise of lasting love. The three trilogies follow Caitlin from her family life at Ryan Acres, to Highgate Academy, the exclusive boarding school in the posh horse country of Virginia, through college, and on to a glamorous career in journalism in New York City.

Don't miss Caitlin!

THE LOVE TRILOGY

☐	24716-6	**LOVING #1**	$3.50
☐	25130-9	**LOVE LOST #2**	$3.50
☐	25295-X	**TRUE LOVE #3**	$3.50